FLESH WITHOUT SOUL

Pochassic

Original and Modified Cover Art by Kasia and CoverDesignStudio.com

ISBN: 1511538511
ISBN 13: 9781511538510

"All concerns of men go wrong when they wish to cure evil with evil." —Sophocles

ACT 1
GENESIS

"Help me Father..." Charlie frantically prayed as the plane began plunging. The thin nineteen-year-old's stomach was once again rising into his chest. "Help me." Turbulence had been his only travelling companion and it was now back with a vengeance. The thunderstorm battering Flight 316—which was making its final approach to Tokyo—was the worst of all the storms that had been chasing him across the globe since he left Massachusetts. The plane at times had shook so hard it made the flight feel like a broken carnival ride that threatened to spin apart.

The lightning flashed with such frequency that it gave the illusion the plane was under attack from antiaircraft fire. Charlie tried cinching his seat belt even tighter around his waist as his torso rocked from side to side. "I can't die now." Charlie released the strap, clasping his armrests with a death grip. Panic suffocated him as he felt the walls of the cabin close in on him. "Please Father." Scared and desperate, his silent prayer erupted out of him. "Please Father. Help me."

"Shhh... honey," the elderly voice said. "I know it's scary..."

Charlie looked to his right. The old woman sitting next to him seemed as though she was on a different flight, her eyes serene, her smile warm.

"We'll be fine," the elderly woman said. She gently stroked the terrified young man's hand and tried to comfort him.

Charlie meekly smiled back and said, "I hate to fly..." A loud banging interrupted the terrified teen's response. A feeling of weightlessness overcame Charlie as he felt the plane plunge and rise underneath him.

"Oh please save me, Father," Charlie said.

"Shhhh," the elderly woman cooed at him again. "It's just a bit of turbulence. This isn't even that bad." The timbre of her voice changed from a parent comforting a scared child to someone gossiping with an old friend. "I remember this one time, over Chicago, it got really bad. People were flying out of their seats. Some even hit the ceiling." She chuckled as she once again patted his hand, which strangled the armrest tighter as she talked.

"You're not helping you crazy old bat..." Charlie thought as the plane continued to lurch up and down like a yo-yo.

"Thank you," he politely responded to the old woman.

Smiling warmly at the teen whose close-cropped hair reminded her of her grandson, the elderly woman asked, "Would it help you if we prayed together? I always find comfort knowing the Lord is here with me." Without waiting for a response, the octogenarian began reciting the Lord's Prayer.

"Our Father, who art in Heaven, hallowed be thy name..." Charlie smiled as she prayed next to him. He followed along in his head and changed certain key words, just as Father had always instructed.

The plane continued to lurch violently as the old woman prayed. The cabin lights flickered in unison with flashes of lightning outside as though engaged in conversation. Charlie heard others on the half-empty red-eye join in on the woman's prayers. As the benediction progressed the plane lurched less and less. The lights stopped their dance with the storm. As the chorus of travelers said "amen," the turbulence finally gave up the ghost.

DING.

"All right everyone." The pilot's Texas accent was calm. "Looks like we've made it through the worst of it." Charlie could hear true relief in the pilot's voice. "We will be landing soon. Please enjoy your stay in beautiful Japan."

Charlie released his death grip on the armrest. As the wheels touched down, squealing and screeching, a cheer arose from the relieved travelers.

"Thank you, Father, for saving me," Charlie said.

"See?" the blue-haired woman asked while petting his hand. "He always answers our prayers."

Charlie smiled back at her and warmly responded, "He certainly does."

⊷⊶

"Welcome to Japan." The Japanese customs agent smiled as she politely addressed Charlie. "May I see your passport?"

"Umm, yes," Charlie said and extended his hand, presenting his passport to the young woman.

"Do you have anything to declare?" she asked as she stamped his virgin passport.

Charlie's mind ran through a few things. "You're hot." "You look like an anime cartoon come to life." And: "You want to fuck? 'Cause seriously, you only have a couple of days to live anyway." He simply smiled warmly at her and said, "No."

"Is your trip business or pleasure, sir?"

"Pleasure, seeing Japan has always been on my bucket list and I am so excited. I'm going to be here for two whole weeks."

"Enjoy your stay, sir." The polite and perfunctory reply came from the thoroughly overworked, overtired, and underpaid woman.

"Thank you," Charlie replied. Walking toward the escalators leading to baggage claim, he felt good inside knowing that soon she would be one with eternity and that she'd be happier there.

Upon stepping off of the escalator, Charlie scanned baggage claim for the men's room all the while mentally running through his checklist. "Objective one: arrive in Japan, check. Objective two..." Recognizing the sign for the men's room Charlie became awash in excitement. He briskly walked toward his destination. "Objective two: extraction."

Culture shock hit Charlie upon entering a stall in the men's room. A computerized armrest on a toilet was not something he had expected. A touch-screen display offered a multitude of options including FLUSH, SPRAY BIDET, FLUSHING SOUND (with volume control), WATER PRESSURE, and POWERFUL DEODORIZER.

Charlie chuckled, thinking about the homeland he would never see again. "Wow, we didn't even lead the world in toilet bowl technology. Father was so right, America sucked."

After closing the door he sat on the toilet with his pants on and reached into his mouth to remove his upper plate of false teeth. Father, in his brilliance, had pulled Charlie's upper teeth and replaced them with false ones he had specially crafted.

Charlie placed the false teeth on his lap and began wiggling the back left molar gently. As he did, the hard ceramic tooth came free. Turning it over, he saw them for the first time.

Where in a real tooth roots would be, this molar had four small plastic vials that he gently removed before replacing the molar and reinserting the upper plate in his mouth.

He took the vials and stared at them. He then put three of the vials in his shirt pocket, keeping one in his clenched fist.

He stood up, pressed the FLUSHING SOUND button, giggled, and then pushed POWERFUL DEODORIZER button. The sickeningly sweet odor immediately gagged him. "Shit smells better than that," he thought.

Exiting the stall it hit him. The enormity of what he was chosen to do. His importance to Father and how much he was truly loved and trusted.

Charlie's nerves kicked in. His body shuddered. His hand trembled. Exiting the men's room Charlie took a deep breath to calm himself. "Objective one: arrive in Japan, check. Objective two: extraction, check." Charlie glanced at his hand, which concealed the small plastic vile. Looking up he saw his bag on the luggage carousel. "Keep up appearances, you don't need it but take it anyway." Walking over he grasped the black suitcase, which was filled with everything a real tourist would have brought.

"Feeling better?"

The friendly voice made Charlie smile as he turned toward the kindly but kind of kooky old lady from the plane.

"I do. Thank you so much, your prayer really helped," Charlie said. He hoped the sarcasm in his head was not leaking out of his throat. "Where are you headed from here?" he asked her, sensing an opportunity.

"I'm going up north. My grandson settled there after marrying a lovely lady he met when he was stationed in Okinawa." She smiled and asked, "And you?"

"Tokyo mostly," Charlie responded and smiled, knowing how much Father loved him to have sent him this woman heading north. "Please let me help you with your bag." Charlie grabbed her suitcase while snapping the concealed vile in his hand. The toxic mutagen felt cool as it began aerosolizing. Just as Father said it would.

"Grandma." A husky male voice bellowed from behind Charlie. Glancing back he saw her grandson and his family approaching.

"Well," Charlie said while putting the elderly woman's luggage down. "Looks like you won't be needing me."

The elderly woman waved at her grandson and replied, "Please wait. I'd like you to meet my family."

"I would be delighted," Charlie said. He clasped his hands together in a gesture of delight. The cool infection cascaded over both his hands.

"Grandma, how was the flight?" her grandson asked. He had a square jaw, close-cropped hair, and perfect posture, and he smiled warmly at the two of them as he approached.

"It was a bit bumpy. I'd like you to meet a friend I met on the plane. We prayed together during turbulence."

"Of course you did," the man replied. Turning toward Charlie, he said warmly, "I'm sorry about that, she prays over everything. I'm Frank, Frank Branches. This is my wife, Kaiyo, and our first-born son, Hajime." He motioned toward his wife and newborn.

Charlie put down his bag and extended his infectious right hand.

"She was lovely," Charlie said. Frank's handshake almost crushed Charlie's—whose hand was now just slightly cool with vaporizing death. "She kept me calm up there." He turned and extended his hand similarly to the man's wife, and finally extended his left hand toward the baby while saying, "Something tells me before you know it." He touched the child's head, mutagen still vaporizing off his fingers, "this one is going to be a real lady-killer."

"It was lovely meeting you," the wife said, clearly trying to move this whole thing along.

"Thank you, I must get going. I have to catch the Narita Express into Tokyo," Charlie said and then turned and walked away. He checked his pocket and felt the remaining vials—he would break these upon arriving at Shinjuku Station in downtown Tokyo, the most populated city on Earth. A feeling of relief washed over him. He held up his cell phone and stopped, pausing to take a touristy-looking selfie in front of a sign that said "Welcome to Japan."

As he walked toward the station he added text to his picture: "dear Father vacation off to a great start, everything going great, easy as 123."

SEND.

"Wow, this is happening." Charlie was giddy. "Objective one: arrival, check. Objective two: extraction check. Objective three: extinction, check."

Charlie felt the warmth of Father's pride washing over him as he strolled toward the subway to downtown Tokyo.

＝＋＋＝

Ding! The sound of an incoming message sent a shiver of excitement through Michael's body. He looked over at his laptop, which was sitting on his messy desk. "This is it," he thought as he raised himself out of his ornate, hand-carved seventeenth-century William and Mary great chair and walked toward his computer. The steel floor was cold on his bare feet as he strode across the room, which was his private sanctuary. He hadn't felt this nervous since the seventh grade when he asked Nancy Nebhetet, the first girl he ever loved, to the spring semiformal dance. His eyes widened as he sat down, opened up his laptop, logged in, and saw the alert flashing in the corner of the screen: "INCOMING MESSAGE FROM: disciple#1." As was his custom when he was nervous, Michael curled his lips into his mouth until the first whiskers from his prematurely silver beard poked at his tongue. He moved the cursor over the alert, clicked on his mouse, and saw what he had been waiting for. An image so beautiful it moved him to tears. He realized he was smiling so wide his face actually hurt slightly. He clasped his hands together, intertwining his fingers, and bowed his head, thinking: "For it is written. Although the soul is pure, the flesh is wicked."

9

He pushed back from the desk, raising his thick frame from the chair, and grabbed a shiny metal container similar in shape and size to a thermos from the top drawer, before heading toward the temple to share the news with his flock, leaving his laptop open to the picture of a smiling Charlie in Japan.

꧁ ꧂

"Pizza's up!" Kara Kerr's melodic voice easily cut through the din of the kitchen. The smells of shaved steak, sizzling onions, and fryolater oil battled with the scent of a perfect pepperoni pizza as Kara and her staff worked feverishly. The prematurely gray, five-foot-two, thirty-six-year-old owner of Kara Mia's Pizzeria began untying the strings of her bright-red apron. "Hey Jaden!" Kara shouted. She was accustomed to having to yell at Jaden, her teenage dishwasher and delivery driver. She had hired the kid, who always came by for a slice after school, after his father had died. She knew the family and knew they needed money. She also knew how hard Jaden was taking his dad's death.

Kara thought she could help the kid out. Give him a safe place to be after school. Maybe fix the kid's life a little. That's just who she was.

"Jaden!"

However, Kara found his ADD—which for some reason appeared to make him deaf—infuriating.

"Yes?" Jaden asked while looking up from the steaming sink, which was foaming with bubbles like a giant rabid dog. He was trying to scrape scorched tomato sauce from the bottom of a deep pot.

"Delivery," Kara said as she slipped off her apron, which was freshly splattered with pizza sauce, and tossed it in the hamper just outside of the kitchen in the hall to her office.

"Whoa. What are you doing?" Jaden had never seen Kara take off her apron before closing time.

"I am leaving early." Kara flashed a smile at the kid. "I am going to my brother's place, he begged me to come by and said he has a surprise birthday gift for me."

Stunned, Jaden replied, "You never take time off. You even came in after the car accident with a broken neck 'cause you said the shop can't run itself."

"First off, I only fractured my collarbone. That is not even close to a broken neck."

"Still it's pretty bad ass," Jaden replied.

"Whatever," Kara shot back, humor tingeing her voice. "Anyway," she continued, "Tommy is going to cover for me." She glanced over at the large Italian pizza cook who was tying up his apron with his thick fingers.

"Wait a second," Jaden said. His mind flashed—her brother? His mouth suddenly spilled out the words, "Isn't your brother in a cult or something?"

Jaden felt his stomach drop knowing he had just inadvertently put his foot in his mouth...yet again.

Kara's friendly face turned icy. Her body tensed visibly. If it had been anyone else in this kitchen—Tommy, the two-hundred-pound pound pizza cook; Joey, the six-foot-three line cook; or any of the other guys who were bigger and stronger than her—they would have been on the ground bleeding by now.

"Hey let's all calm down over here," Tommy said, remembering the last time someone had done something bad to Kara's family. A customer had spit on the picture hanging near the register of Jane, Kara's sister, graduating from basic training in her navy uniform. The clearly drunk woman then began calling Kara's sister something along the lines of a baby killer. Tommy did not want a repeat of that bloody fiasco that almost cost all of them their jobs. "Jaden is an idiot, he didn't mean that."

Jaden, looking meek, nodded in agreement. "I am so sorry. I really am."

Kara breathed slowly and softly responded, "I know," and then let out a long breath.

"See. All good," Tommy said and turned toward Kara. "And don't worry about a thing while you're gone. I've got it all down, even schedules." Tommy abruptly stopped speaking. He felt his heart drop.

"Schedules?" Kara cautiously replied. She had told Tommy to cover for a few hours during the usual after-dinner lull. Yet his reply seemed to indicate that she was going to be gone for a while.

"Umm, yeah," Tommy said. "You know...I...umm know not to touch them. That's all I meant. You should go have a good time now."

Kara saw the sweat forming on Tommy's upper lip the way it always did when he was bluffing during the staff's Sunday night poker game. Tommy couldn't keep a secret to save his life. Smelling blood in the water, Kara verbally moved in to break Tommy.

"Maybe I should stay," Kara said in a slightly melancholic tone. "I'll call Michael and tell him I don't think you can cover for me tonight."

"Oh god no! Don't do that!" Tommy was a big guy. But Michael was bigger, and like everyone in the Kerr family he had a startling capacity for violence. "You're going on a cruise," Tommy said, blurting out the secret that he had promised Michael he would keep confidential. "I'm covering till you get back, which will be before payroll, so there won't be a problem..." he swallowed nervously. "Covering for you was sort of...going to be my birthday gift. You deserve some fun, boss." Tommy felt awful. He ruined the surprise. He was in trouble. He knew she would be ecstatic that Michael would go to such lengths for her. He also knew if he didn't get her to go he would face Michael's wrath. Crazy people are not people you want to fight with.

Kara beamed thinking about how much trouble Michael had gone through for her. Normally she would never take off time from the restaurant. But Kara loved surprises. She was overwhelmed that her baby brother would go to such lengths for her.

"You know what?" she said as she looked at Tommy's ever-increasingly anxious face. "I'm going." Her smile lit up the kitchen. She turned to Jaden and said, "My brother's a hippy that hangs out in the woods with his friends smoking a lot of pot. That's not a cult, it's called a commune or a cabal or something like that."

"I'm wicked sorry," Jaden replied. He was still nervous that his boss was mad at him.

"I know, kid," Kara said. Happiness surged through her system like a drug. She looked at Tommy and winked as she grabbed her coat. She unwittingly skipped a step as she headed toward the exit of her restaurant, excitement bubbling up in her soul.

"Tommy," she said, stopped at the entrance, and looked back at her employee. "Thank you."

A broad smile crossed Tommy's lips. "After all you've done for me over the years it's the least I could do. Now get out of here and go have some fun."

"Hey Tommy." Kara felt like playing with him a little more "Where am I going? The Caribbean? Central America? Where?"

"You're going on a boat. After that I can gladly say I don't know." Thankful Michael had not told him anything else.

"Bye." Kara smiled, then left. The nighttime blast of snowy New England air that hit her face wiped away the warm aroma of the pizza shop, that one neighborhood kid had told her smelled like Little League victories.

—<+ +>—

Kara sat down behind the wheel of her pickup truck, lit a menthol cigarette, and brought her vehicle to life with a turn of the ignition. Even though she was thrilled to be going on vacation, she still felt bad about scaring the kid like that, then laughed to herself thinking if her sister Jane had been there Jaden would currently be in a hospital intensive care ward. "Probably having to eat through a straw the rest of his life." Smiling, her mind shifted gears to her brother.

"I am so happy!" Kara bounced with excitement in the seat of her car. She was so hopeful, as she traversed the snowy night, that her brother might be getting a little more normal, or at least a little less whacko.

He was always weird, but it wasn't until he dropped out of his PhD program in bioengineering that he really turned a corner. To Kara he was still her goofy, but weird, little brother. To their mother, he became anathema. A traitor to the family that had sacrificed so much to send him to the best schools, only to have him throw it all away just as he was reaching the zenith of his education.

"And for what!" Kara could still hear her mother screaming at him. "You did what!" Her voice echoed in Kara's memory. "You threw away everything for what again?!? I want to hear this again because I must be going crazy, because I did not hear you say what I thought I heard!!!"

Kara's memory then replayed her brother's meek reply: "I found God."

"Really?!?!" her mother bellowed. "Where was he? Behind the couch? Maybe hiding in the closet. Hey Jesus, how 'bout coming out of the closet?"

"It's my duty to serve God, and I didn't say it was Jesus," her brother had furiously replied.

It just went on from there. Around and around, feelings being hurt, everyone screaming, no one listening. And as always, Kara had been in the middle of it all, trying in vain to keep the peace.

Her baby brother wasn't well. She knew that. But he wasn't some evil psycho the way mom had made him out to be. He was her blood. She knew that all you had to do was be patient with him. She was sure he would come around to his senses eventually.

And even if he never did, he was still blood. Her blood. And she would never turn her back on him.

Taking a long drag on her cigarette, she turned on the truck's radio. Classic rock always helped center her whenever she started to think too much about the past. The chorus of her favorite old Elvis Costello song blasted through the speakers. She exhaled the cigarette smoke out the slightly open window. At the top of her lungs she began bellowing along with the chorus: "What's so funny 'bout peace, love, and understanding?".

THA-THUNK!

The jolt of hitting a pothole the size of a moon crater rattled Kara's teeth. "Really Westfield?" she fumed at her hometown. "Why? Why? Why can't you fix the fuckin' potholes! This city has been here since 1669 and no one has figured out how to pave a fuckin' street"

THA-THUNK!

Kara couldn't wait to get through downtown, with its dull red-brick buildings housing bars, liquor stores, and rival pizza shops.

THA-THUNK

Not to mention the worst-maintained roads in all of New England.

Kara passed by the steel-framed black clock tower and a smile crossed her lips. She always thought it was funny the town couldn't afford to pave the roads, but they somehow were able to afford this weird clock tower with the Roman numeral four misprinted as "IIII" instead of "IV." Kara also loved the rumors that the mayor bought the misprinted clock for a discount and pocketed the rest of the cash. "Gotta love stupid conspiracy theories." She thought as she drove past the timepiece and over the eastbound bridge of the twin iron bridges spanning the Westfield River. A quick left past the tattoo parlor and she was on her way into the hills where her brother loved living.

One cigarette later, Kara turned down the dirt road to her brother's house at the base of Tekoa Mountain. The loose pebbles hitting the underside of her car sounded like she was under attack by the residents of Lilliput. There were two things Kara disliked about her brother's place. One was this desolate dirt road. The second and more important thing was the rattlesnake population, or the "neighbors" as her brother liked to call them. Using the jagged granite caves of Tekoa as breeding grounds, Michael's reptilian neighbors usually kept to themselves, but their presence precluded any housing developments from happening near the picturesque peak. Their presence also precluded Kara visiting her brother in the summertime.

Michael's cottage came into view. A small gray shack with small wisps of white smoke rising from the chimney. Her brother was waiting for her on the rickety wooden porch. His large frame, his full silver beard, and his flowing silver locks glowed as they were lit up by her headlights. Kara thought it was funny how the 'Kerr curse' as her mom called the family's gray hair made her brother look more and more like Santa Claus every year. Kara parked her car, opened her door, and walked up to her brother, who was waiting with open arms for his usual embrace.

"It is so good to see you, Michael," Kara said warmly as she hugged her six-foot-two, 220-pound "little" brother. "You look good."

"Thank you," Michael responded, "You look great, too. Pizzeria still doing well?" His eyes twinkled as he looked at Kara.

"Can't complain. Well actually, I could, but what the hell's the point of that?" She chuckled.

"So I have a very special gift for you," Michael said as he stared at his favorite family member. "Are you excited?"

"Yes I am! I am so excite—"

A gloved hand was suddenly covering her mouth. Kara tried to scream—a sound of muffled terror was all that could escape from her. The thick, muscled arm constricted her chest like a python, pinning her against the unseen attacker behind her. She shot her hands back trying to gouge out her assailant's eyes. Two men in white robes emerged from Michael's cabin, each grabbing at one of Kara's arms—she hit one square in his nose, baptizing his face with his own blood, before he got control of her limb. Kara viciously kicked at her attackers, trying to break the knees of the men on either side of her.

"Grab her legs!" Michael screamed at Kara's attackers.

Kara's eyes shot to her brother. He was smiling. Betrayal, confusion, terror, all spinning in her brain like a tornado.

"Please Kara, don't struggle." Her brother admonished the woman whose muffled screams filled the quiet, snowy air. "I'm sorry but this is going to hurt."

Kara saw Michael moving toward her, his right hand holding the largest needle and syringe she had ever seen. Michael rolled up her sleeve. "HOLD HER STILL!" he barked at the large men, who were still struggling to contain the woman. "Please Kara, this will hurt a lot less if you stop squirming." Michael implored his sibling as he moved the needle to her arm. "I SAID HOLD HER STILL!" he barked at the white-robed attackers. Clamping one hand on her forearm, his lips curled into a sadistic smile. Michael pierced her flesh with the long, thick needle.

"OH MY GOD NO! NO! WHAT ARE YOU DOING GOD NO!" Kara's thoughts screamed as the needle entered her. Michael's thumb pressed down on the plunger, scorching Kara's veins. Fire began coursing through her bloodstream.

"Shhh. It's almost over now." Michael's calm tone was that of a parent telling a child only one more spoonful of medicine and you'll be done. Kara's muffled screams became muffled sobs. "Good." Michael praised his sister as he pulled the empty syringe away from her arm. "So that was everyone else's gift. This, however,"

Michael continued as he picked up another syringe, "this is your gift. Now, there are a few temporary side effects. Including paralysis, but that wears off within a few days."

THWACK!

Michael plunged the thick needle straight into her chest like a serial killer dispatching a victim. Kara's vision began growing dark around the edges.

"It also contains a sedative." Michael's voice sounded distant to Kara, realizing she was losing consciousness. "Why?" was the last thought her brain could muster before darkness enveloped her.

⋙ ⋘

Kara eyelids slowly fluttered open as she regained consciousness. Thoughts sloshed slowly through her awakening mind. "I'm sitting?" she thought. "Why am I waking up sitting?"

The smell of stale cleaning chemicals mixed with traces of urine filled her lungs. "Dr. Lee?" Her family veterinarian's office was the closest smell her groggy mind could connect to the sanitized stench coating her throat. "No...a hospital." Her eyes felt dry as she blinked hard to refocus them in the fluorescent lighting. "I must be in a hospital. Wait...did Michael...no, that can't be right... Michael never would have..." As the reflection from the shiny steel wall in front of Kara came into focus, her internal debate froze, along with her blood.

Kara was still in her street clothes. She saw the thick leather strap securing her forehead to the headrest of the wheelchair she was sitting in, which had matching straps that were locking her legs and arms into place. A single piece of duct tape fastened her lips shut. Tubes ran from her arm up to an IV bag that was slowly dripping a clear liquid into her bloodstream.

"You son of a bitch!" The anger that flooded Kara was primal. So was her body's response. Every nerve synapse fired, every muscle tensed, every part of her struggled to get out of her trap. "Nothing?"

"MOVE!" Again and again her mind screamed for her body to respond to no avail.

Fury slowly faded to fear as Kara realized the straps weren't the only thing holding her down. She looked down to her left hand, which was lying on the wheelchair's armrest, just beyond the leather shackle that was binding her wrist. "Move!" her mind haplessly scolded her unresponsive fingers. Her memory reached backward to the attack. "Paralysis, he said I would be paralyzed." Her thoughts were coming quicker now. "I'd be paralyzed...four days? No, two, maybe three." The attack became clearer in her memory as the cobwebs cleared from her mind.

"Father!" the sound of the excited female voice shattered the silence of the room. Kara's nervous system sent signals to leap that went unheeded by her hibernating muscles. The reflection Kara stared at now was a young woman, twentyish, and garbed in the same white robes as Kara's attackers. The woman's hair was bleached almost to the platinum hue of Kara's own.

"She is risen!" the woman bellowed. "She is risen." Still yelling, the woman ran out of Kara's line of sight.

"C'mon, move!" Kara's mind screamed at her unresponsive muscles. "MOVE!"

She could hear hurried footsteps, sandals slapping against a steel floor. It was getting louder. "MOVE!"

Thunderous applause filled Kara's ears. Four men also adorned with white robes, clapping wildly, entered the room along with the blonde that Kara thought looked like a younger version of herself.

Kara watched the reflection on the wall as the young blonde doppelganger approached her from behind. The woman was all smiles—she grabbed the handles of the wheelchair and spun Kara around. The steel room flashed by quickly—medical posters, test tubes, and then four empty-eyed, white-robed, smiling men, applauding her as though she were a toddler who just blew out her birthday candles.

"Hallelujah she has risen" Michael's voice boomed out from behind the men smiling at Kara.

"Oh my God," Kara thought as the men parted to allow her brother entry, black-and-gold robes draped over his large frame. His face beaming with pride underneath his thick silver beard and long platinum locks that threatened to swallow his face. In each hand he held a dead-looking snake. "My brother isn't in a cult." Her thoughts dripping with despair. "He runs a cult."

Raising his hands over his head, revealing two thick brown rattlesnakes, one clutched in each meaty hand, the sound of their rattling echoing off the metal walls. "For the sister of God has finally joined the righteous ones." His tone was boisterous and triumphant. "Evil shall soon pass from this Earth, my children. Evil shall soon pass forever from the face of this twisted world."

The eyes of the men standing on either side of her brother well up—tears stream down their cheeks as they kneel down before him, reverently reaching out to touch the silk robe adorning her brother.

"It is time for the crucible of *Crotalus horridus,*" Michael said, his eyes twinkling in the fluorescent lighting. "Shelbi." Michael addressed the woman behind his sister's wheelchair.

"Yes Father?"

"Bring her for final judgment."

Kara knew as the wheel squeaked underneath her that she was about to die.

⊷┼┼⊶

"Hrii Hupadgh L'chae'im." The guttural chant the cult had begun as the procession entered a brightly lit steel hallway was unintelligible to Kara. "Gof'nn Sll'haa N'gha Ph'shugg." However, the slow cadence of the chant she instantly recognized as a funeral dirge. "Oh God I don't want to die." She felt fear choking her as Michael danced in front of the robed men on either side of Kara and Shelbi pushed her at what seemed to be a snail's pace.

The two snakes Michael held in each hand looked more dead than alive as they flopped like pieces of thick rope—only their rattles seemed fully awake as they flickered violently.

"Oh sister, my dear sister." The chanting and the movement of the congregation stopped the instant Michael spoke. Walking slowly back toward his immobilized sister he addresses her: "You were always there for me. You never failed me. I love you with all my heart and soul." His tone loving and genuine.

The cult surrounding Kara responded robotically in unison: "As do we all."

Michael extended his arms straight out, allowing the snakes' heads to dangle inches from Kara's eyes. Their black-and-blue forked tongues flickered at the air so close to Kara that she felt a slight breeze brush by her eyes.

"Entrance is granted," Michael bellowed while withdrawing the reptiles from his sister's face. He danced back a few steps, stopped, and then bowed toward his bound sibling. Stepping to the side of the hallway, he revealed an ancient arched door with red paint saturating its oak timbers—it was wholly out of place when compared to the metal rooms and hallways Kara had seen. This portal belonged in a medieval cathedral, not here. Shelbi stepped out from behind the wheelchair, walked over to the entryway, and swung it open. The stench blasting out from behind the door was overwhelming. Paralysis prevented Kara from gagging on the taste of urine that coated her airway.

"Oh my God." Kara was thunderstruck by what was beyond the archway before her. "I'm underground."

The cave before Kara was immense and so was the sound of an untold number of snakes violently vibrating their rattles. The quartz and mica walls danced from the light of candles, hundreds of them arranged throughout the subterranean cavity. As the venomous reptiles slithered through the crevices that scarred the cavern's walls, their scales caught and reflected glimpses of candlelight. They entered the huge chamber. There was an altar—a black stalagmite with Michael's face carved into it with a long, inclining stone pathway leading up to it. Kara saw stalagmites scattered throughout the cavern floor on either side of the sloping runway.

"Today we ask for one last blessing for my beloved sister Kara." Michael's voice easily boomed out louder than the cacophony of vipers that filled his unholy temple. The procession halted at the sound of their leader's words. Michael strode out in front of Kara. His hands, no longer holding snakes, rose over his head. "The blessing of the vipers separates the righteous from the unworthy."

Kara felt the cool scales of snakes slithering across her neck. Shelbi, standing behind her, was ritualistically draping snakes across the back of the captive woman's neck—after a moment, she began carefully placing more vipers across Kara's shoulders.

As the cool reptilian scales of the snakes cascaded across her neck and the sounds of their rattling mingled with the rhythmic clapping of the cult members behind her, she was no longer afraid. She was pissed.

"I don't care what it takes," her thoughts snarling in her head, "I am going to get out of this! And I am going to kill you!" It was a primal instinctive thought, matched only in intensity to the look of pure hatred emanating from the bound woman's eyes that was directed squarely at her brother, who, oblivious to Kara's death stare, danced around basking in his followers' adoration.

DING! The incoming message alert sounded on Michael's laptop. "INCOMING MESSAGE FROM: disciple#1." Michael never saw Charlie's last message he sent before bleeding to death from bite wounds.

Following the blessing of the serpent ceremony, Michael had ordered everyone to leave the huge cavern so he could tell his beloved sister what was about to unfold in private. Shelbi had entered Michael's sanctuary as she often did when she knew he was busy. It was Shelbi who opened disciple#1's message:

"FATHER HELP ME!! THEY ATTACKED SOME R FAST ! BBLEEDING REALLY BAD ! HELP ME FATER SHOTS NOTSTOP ATTACK."

Shelbi's slender index finger clicked on the mouse, deleting Charlie's dying plea for mercy and help to his deity.

"Shots don't stop attacks, Charlie?" Her tone was dismissive "It's an antidote not a repellant you idiot." Shelbi—certain and happy that Charlie would soon be dead—rushed out of Michael's lair and toward the communication center, or as she like to call it, the war room, with an excited smile gracing her lips.

❦

Michael watched the last follower exit the temple and close the ancient timber door before addressing his sister.

"It's fine," he said assuredly as he began picking the snakes off his sister. "It never goes above fifty degrees down here. They never get aggressive or strike. Just rattle their tales hoping you'll leave them alone."

"Oh," Kara thought, "that makes it all better you piece of shit!"

"When we were building the bunker we hit into this cave system," Michael said, his voice brimming with pride as he removed the last reptile. "It's huge. We reinforced some of it with steel like my lab and living quarters." Having cleared his sister of snakes,

Michael now sat before Kara with his legs folded like a pretzel beneath him. He looked up at his wheelchair-bound sister. Grinning from ear to ear, he began to explain.

"I'm so sorry! Please don't be mad. I had to save your life." He placed his hands upon her feet. "The world is a vile and wretched place. It is time for it to end. It is time for it to be reborn." Michael's hands rose from his sister's feet to above his head. "To be reborn in my image."

"I AM GOING TO KILL YOU." Kara was staring daggers at her sibling while screaming inside her head, "HOW COULD YOU DO THIS TO ME? I'M YOUR SISTER YOU FUCKING LUNATIC!"

Michael was sure he saw thankfulness in Kara's eyes. "I knew you couldn't stay mad at me," he said. His tone was playful. Patting her feet again, he rose to his own feet and said, "This will be easier to show you then to explain all the technical stuff." Michael was also sure his sister wasn't smart enough to understand gene sequencing and DNA manipulation. So he tried to keep the explanations simple for her as he began wheeling her toward the doorway.

"You see, sister, nature has a way of balancing things out." He paused dramatically at the end of each sentence, wanting to give his sister time to drink in the brilliance of his words.

"Fuck you!" his sister replied in thought.

"There is this brilliant fungi I discovered during my PhD work," Michael said.

"Great, tell me about your fungus," Kara thought.

"*Ophiocordyceps destructans*, I discovered it. It's amazing," Michael said. He stopped pushing Kara to swing open the heavy wooden door leading to the steel corridor, then continued: "It is basically nature's population control system." Michael smiled at his sister, mistaking her glowering for rapt fascination of his brilliance. He stepped behind his sister and pushed her down the brightly lit passage. "I improved it...well, the technical term would be *weaponized* it."

"What the fuck is he saying?" Kara—no less furious—began listening more to her brother's deranged ramblings.

"I did what everyone said was impossible. I was able to cross the fungi with an airborne virus." The pride he felt at his brilliance caused tears to well up in his eyes. Wiping the tears away, he pushed Kara past the lab she woke up in and toward a new doorway. "The fungi's DNA was manipulated with the DNA of the rhinopharyngitis virus, better known to the less educated as the common cold." Arriving at the steel doorway, Michael opened the portal and wheeled his sister into his communication center. Shelbi seemed surprised as they entered the room.

━❖ ❖━

"What are you doing in here?" Michael's tone seemed tinged with suspicion to Kara

"I had a vision of Charlie smiling, just now, in my room," Shelbi said. Kara could tell that Shelbi was clearly lying. "I came in here to see if our seed had borne fruit."

"Don't just stand there. Turn on the power," Michael said. He clearly had no clue that he was being lied to.

Shelbi opened up the circuit breaker door on the far wall and flipped a few switches. The wall of old LCD monitors flickered to life.

Michael left Kara parked in front of the monitors as he began fumbling for a remote in a desk drawer just behind her. The wall was eight feet tall by twelve feet wide, every inch of which was covered with flat-screen monitors. As they came on Kara saw they were all tuned to foreign news stations. Unintelligible crawls streamed across the muted screens as news anchors bleated out various stories of local importance.

"HE DID IT!" Shelbi gushed while pointing to a monitor in the upper right-hand corner of the wall. Kara looked to where she was pointing.

The aerial footage on the screen took Kara's breath away: huge buildings engulfed in flames; thick black smoke choking the sky. Michael pressed the mute button, marrying sound to the images of horror unfolding on live TV.

While the language the newscaster spoke was completely unintelligible to Kara, the footage of people running in the streets brought her back to that September morning when she turned on her television and witnessed people fleeing for their lives as New York tumbled down upon them.

"I love you," Shelbi said to Michael. Her tone implied she was much closer to Kara's brother than anyone else in his flock, as did the quick glance she shot Kara. "Shall I gather the others?" Shelbi's eyes, refocused on Michael, now stared at him adoringly.

"Yes, please." Michael's tone was hushed. "Have them enter quietly. After all this is a sacred moment."

Kara was barely aware of Shelbi leaving as she sat transfixed by the images of mayhem before her. It looked a lot like 9/11 footage, except there wasn't one single event people were running from, like the collapsing towers. The entire population of this city on fire appeared to be attacking one another in the streets.

"It took God six days to give birth to this vile and wicked world," Michael said as he muted the broadcast and stared unblinkingly at the images of carnage before him. "I'm going to kill it," he said, his lips curling into a smile under his thick silver beard as he spoke. "It'll take me about a week to infect it. Approximately six or seven weeks after that and voila..." He turned to his meet his sister's eyes. "This wicked and evil world will soon be dead and forgotten."

Michael kneeled down and whispered in his sister's ear, "I saved you from that." He motioned to the Japanese newscast. "In nature the fungi only attack ant colonies that have grown too large to be sustainable for the surrounding habitat." His was voice brimming with pride. "The fungi sickens a few ants, kills them, then it manipulates the insect's central nervous system, reanimating the corpse, causing it to attack other members of the colony. Thus spreading the infection. " Leaning over, he kissed his sister on top of her head, then continued. "I modified it to attack humans. Except of course for those of you who have been inoculated against it."

"Oh my God, Michael! What have you done?" Kara felt nauseous as she listened to her brother continue.

"The 'gift,'" Michael said, "as I like to call it, spreads like wildfire. First you think you have a mild cold, nothing more serious than the sniffles. Then after three days you die and the fungi uses your corpse to attack any human still alive."

The images on the screen were getting worse as Michael kept explaining to Kara what he had done. The video had switched from aerial shots to cell phone video of the catastrophe. After seeing the new footage, Michael unmuted the screen. The newscaster's words were unintelligible to both Kara and Michel, but his fear transcended language as he spoke.

The crisp digital footage showed street-level fighting. Riot police were firing live ammunition as a staggering mob approached—chest cavities exploded as bullets tore through the rioters, who stumbled back a few steps before lurching forward unaffected by the gaping chest wounds that should have killed them.

The mob slowly moved toward the police. Some of the infected individuals fell as a barrage of bullets cut the corpses in half. Those gunned down, undeterred by the minor loss of their legs, continued crawling toward their prey. An ear-piercing scream preceded the camera phone panning to the left to see a police officer being shredded as pallid corpses tore flesh from bone with their teeth.

The screams were the worst sounds Kara had ever heard. Until the recipients of Michael's "gift" responded to the policeman's shriek with a sound unlike any she had ever heard. The camera then panned to the right and caught several of the ghouls darting out from the pack. Shrieking and hissing, they leapt toward the police. Two were cut down instantly by head shots that sent their brain matter splattering across the street. One of the corpses got to his target. The man's riot helmet flew off as he tumbled backward— the creature on top of him ripped and swallowed chunks of his neck on the way down.

"Father." The male voice sounded unsure of itself. Michael's flock had entered the room so quietly neither Kara nor Michael had noticed. "Why are some of them...moving fast?"

Kara shifted her focus from the television to her brother. A single bead of sweat ran down from Michael's hairline across his temple, disappearing into his beard. At that moment Kara knew Michael's plan was spinning out of his control.

"Proximity, my child." Michael's voice was confident as he turned to face his flock. "When those with the 'gift' get close to their prey they sometimes have a quick burst of speed. It's common when the *Eciton burchellii* species of South American army ant becomes infected."

"Then why are those other ones moving fast?"

Michael turned around to see the image had again switched to an aerial view. A mass of people were fleeing as hundreds of other people seemed to be chasing them. "Those are people fleeing their fate," Michael dismissively replied. "The infected swarm is what they are running from." The image did show a much larger horde in slow pursuit. However, some of the people Michael claimed were fleeing the slow horde were clearly attacking people who they caught up with.

"But Father..."

"They fell," Michael said, sternly cutting off his follower. "Those people fell, that's all."

The aerial image zoomed out to show that the people fleeing for their lives were about to run into a larger pack converging from two side streets. As the staggering mass of corpses began filling in the crowd's escape route, the fast pursuers slowed down and began to encircle the humans.

Kara, transfixed by the terror unfolding on live TV, realized what Michael didn't. "The fast ones," she thought, "are herding those people into the swarm."

She was right. The fast ones attacked any humans trying to break out of the intersection they were trapped in. Once the slow ones came close enough so there was no escape for the terrified mass of humanity, the fast ones slipped back into the horde, allowing their slower brethren to begin feasting on living flesh.

"Shelbi," Michael said, his voice booming, "bring my sister to my sanctuary." He paused for effect, and then—with every ounce of menace his voice could muster—continued: "I... have a discipline issue to deal with."

"Absolutely, Father," Shelbi said and immediately grasped Kara's wheelchair. Heading toward the door, she shot an accusatory look at the doubting Thomas in her midst, as if saying, "That was the last mistake you will ever make."

⟞⟊⟊⟝

DING!

DING!

DING!

The alerts on Michael's laptop were coming in rapid succession as Shelbi wheeled Kara into her brother's lair.

DING!

"Hear that?" Shelbi asked the paralyzed woman as they entered the room. "That, my dear sister, is the death of this world and the birth of a new one."

Shelbi sat in front of the computer and positioned Kara next to her so as to have a clear view of the screen. The old LCD showed a line of alerts all bearing the name "disciple" followed by a hashtag and number.

"You really should have seen this place when we were fully staffed." Shelbi was trying to make small talk with the unresponsive woman next to her. "There's only a few of us left here, including you of course. Everyone else has gone out to spread the *gift*." Shelbi scrolled through dozens of messages whose taglines included "Moscow is Beautiful" and "Cairo is Amazing." "London is Everything I hoped." "I'm in a New York state of mind." "Washington DC!! I LOVE 'MERICA."

"It's amazing." Shelbi smiled from ear to ear and turned toward Kara. "Father decided to fully infect Japan first. He said it was to inflict maximum psychological trauma on the world." Leaning closer to Kara, she whispered, "I think it's because he loves Godzilla movies so much. He wanted to destroy Japan first. As a sign of respect to his childhood hero."

"Well," Kara thought, "she does know my brother."

"But," Shelbi whispered, "that's just between us." She nudged Kara's leather-bound arm with her elbow.

"Don't fucking touch me!" Kara's thoughts roared, sending waves of endorphins and adrenaline through her incapacitated frame.

"Your brother is a not just a genius. He is God. He inoculated all of us against the infection. Except of course..." Shelby said and turned toward the screen. "Himself."

Kara felt her pinky involuntarily jump on her right hand.

"Oh my God, I just moved." Kara's ears pounded with the blood coursing through them. She wondered if Shelbi had seen her finger move. Fear rose in her throat.

"Short-term plan: destroy the world. Should take no more than a week or two," Shelbi said. She had not noticed Kara's flinch. "Long-term plan: repopulate the world. All of it under one beautiful and glorious religion."

"Wiggle your toes," Kara thought as Shelbi evangelized. "She can't see that." Kara's toes squirmed slowly in her shoes.

"Much like a reverse Noah's Ark, they left here two by two, except Charlie," Shelbi said and smiled. "He was our canary in the coal mine, so to speak. After releasing the gift, they hunker down till it's over, then once it's safe, we start repopulating the world. It might take generations before our descendants finally contact one another." Shelbi turned, her eyes imploring Kara to comprehend the magnitude of Michael's plan. "But when they do, whatever differences they might have shall dissipate into the ether when they realize they all worship the same beautiful and loving God, Michael the Father."

Part of Kara was sure the intensity in Shelbi's eyes signaled she was becoming aware that Kara's paralysis was wearing off. "Calm down. She doesn't suspect anything," Kara thought. "She's just crazy." After having convinced herself that Shelbi's stare was the result of fundamentalist fervor, she began slowly testing her recovery. She tensed and relaxed her muscles, and her body finally began to wake.

"All the people of the world will be united under Michael the Father," Shelbi said. Her voice was inflected with love. "He who rid the world of wickedness." Michael's loud voice joined with Shelbi's as he walked into the room. The sound of the door closing echoed off the steel walls. "He who showed us the evil of flesh without soul." Kara's peripheral vision picked up Michael's hands as they reached out toward Shelbi's neck. "Knowing that one day all his children shall find one another and peace shall reign forevermore." Kara listened to the duet as she saw her brother's hands wrap gently around the back of Shelbi's neck. "Upon this world, which Michael has given unto thee. Amen."

Michael's hands moved down toward his disciple's shoulders. As he rubbed them, he leaned over, gently kissing the top of the zealot's head. His voice sounded both determined and despairing to his sister as he said to the women, "It's just the three of us now."

Michael never fit in as a child. Prodigies rarely do, even in schools for the gifted, Michael did not blend. Distrustful of those he did not know, he took the slightest joke, wisecrack, or ribbing as a great personal offense. The other children always found Mikey to be an angry jerk who really knew how to throw a punch.

Michael was kicked out of three schools during the long, hard years of his education. Michael wasn't just gifted with brilliance of mind. He, like both of his sisters, had a startling capacity for violence.

"Oh no!" Shelbi said. She sounded heartbroken. "They chose wrong?"

"They asked to leave after my judgment on the nonbeliever," Michael said. He was clearly grief-stricken. "They made me kill them. I really didn't want to."

"Shhh. It's OK." Shelbi's sympathy was palpable. "But on the other hand," she said, changing the tone of her voice in an effort to cheer Michael up, "at least we can stop pretending the rattle-snakes are sacred."

They both broke out in the kind of sad laughter heard at funerals, when people fondly share remembrances of the deceased guest of honor.

"The doubter wouldn't listen to reason," Michael continued, still sad, but clearly not nearly as despondent as he seemed moments earlier. "So I snapped his neck, and threw him to the reptiles." Michael sighed. "The others were upset. Some said some very disparaging things to me, which I won't repeat in front of you lovely ladies." Then, as if a switch was flipped inside his head, all semblance of sorrow suddenly left Michael's voice. Anger flavored his inflection as he continued. "They attacked me." His voice grew more indignant with each word. "Those three heretics attacked me." Fire grew in Michael's eyes as did the volume of his tirade. "Me! They attacked me! After all I had done for them, they repay me with doubt and disbelief," Michael said and paused, taking a deep breath before coldly stating, "so I killed them."

Michael's voice once again dripped with despair. He felt despondent about the fact that his followers had driven him to murder. "I loved them." All traces of anger had left Michael. His voice quavered and his tone was heart broken. "Why? Why did they make me kill them?"

"I think," Shelbi said while looking up at the murderer whose hands were still caressing her shoulders, "it's time for your neuroleptics." Shelbi preferred to call her homemade antipsychotic medications by their scientific moniker. It upset Michael less that way. Shelbi's arm extended up, offering a handful of pills to her lover.

"Thank you," Michael quickly replied and snatched the pills out of Shelbi's hand.

"I'm going up to get some lye out of the shed," Shelbi said, trying not to show her disgust as Michael swallowed the pills dry—this particular habit of downing pills without water always made Shelbi sympathy-gag a little. "It'll help dissolve the bodies quickly," she said. "Wouldn't want the snakes getting sick." She moved quickly for the door—Michael's pill-popping made her want to dry heave, which was not going to happen in front of her lover and her God.

Kara intently listened to Shelbi's footsteps. Five steps to the door.

Michael sat at the computer and tried to quietly clear his throat of the chalky taste left by the homemade pharmaceuticals.

Kara heard the door open—three more steps followed by another door being swung open.

"She is amazing," Michael said without averting his eyes from the laptop. "Couldn't have accomplished any of this without her."

Kara's thoughts raced. "Only three steps outside this room." Kara heard a thud.

Michael's concern was etched on his face. He leaped from his chair and raced into the hallway. "Are you OK?"

"I'm good," Shelbi replied. "Hard carrying a twenty-five-pound bag down a ladder. It slipped."

"Here, I'll help you," Michael said.

"Don't worry," Shelbi replied as she swung the bag over her shoulder and winked at Michael. "I'm kind of a badass." They both laughed.

Kara's thoughts ricocheted through her head. "It's close," she thought. "Only three steps outside of this room is the exit." Kara felt hope. "I have a shot at this." Escape now seemed possible to the bound woman. She had the upper hand. "They don't know you can move." Her heart began racing with excitement instead of terror. "They have to unstrap you eventually. Hit them and run." Kara remembered her sister Jane talking about military tactics over Thanksgiving dinner. "It's all about surprise. Hit your enemy when they don't expect it." Kara's hope suddenly switched to guilt, then fear, realizing she had no idea where her sister Jane was stationed, or if she would ever see her again.

⇥⊹ ⊹⇥

"Let's go watch some TV," Michael's booming voice triumphantly sang as he reentered his lair. "My favorite show is on." The wheelchair that Kara was bound to squeaked slightly as Michael lurched it away from his desk. "It's called I'm God." Michael knew his sister. He knew how much she loved him for saving her from his apocalypse. He was positive letting her see the end unfold on live television could only enhance her respect and admiration for him.

As they entered the hallway, Kara, out of the corner of her eye, saw that the entranceway to Michael's lair had been left open by Shelbi. As they moved past it toward the communication center Kara could smell the crisp December air that wafted through the portal. "The surface must be close."

"I am immortal." Michael loved the smell of fresh air. "I'm going to reign supreme on this planet forevermore as its only true deity." The wheelchair lurched to the left and they were back in the communication center.

Kara began to feel light-headed as she was once again wheeled before the banks of monitors.

"It's better just to watch the majesty of my apocalypse unfold before you." Michael's eyes widened as he saw the images of destruction dance across the flickering screens. "What is happening today in Japan will soon happen everywhere."

Michael pulled up a chair next to his sister. He leaned over and kissed his sister on the cheek. "This is going to be epic."

Kara's head was now swimming with the violence—her eyes were drinking it in. Her light-headedness was swiftly moving toward unconsciousness.

Michael's smile started to fade as he scanned the TV screens.

"There you are." Shelbi's voice sounded distant to Kara as she entered the room. "How are things going?"

"I think," Michael said with a wink as he looked at Shelbi, "it's time for some popcorn."

"I can't believe this!" Shelbi yelled at the television screens as she snuggled with Michael, a large bowl of popcorn sitting on his lap. "Are they brain-dead?"

"Of course they are brain-dead." Michael responded. "It's twenty-four-hour cable news. What did you expect?"

"I expected better than this. The world is ending, you'd think they might want to cover it." Shelbi shook her head as she grabbed a handful of the perfectly salted and buttered popcorn and began eating.

Stations around the globe had switched over to the carnage in Japan. Flames, violence, and destruction danced across the screens. The orgy of death gripping Japan was ubiquitous on every channel except for the American ones. On those screens vapid-looking, square-jawed news readers babbled on about a former child actress's raunchy new role, a movie star making a dying child's final wish come true, and a pair of baby koala bears debuting at the San Diego Zoo.

"Oooh, there..." Shelbi said and pointed toward one American station. "BREAKING NEWS" flew across the screen. "Turn it up."

Michael grabbed the remote and unmuted the twenty-four-hour "news leader," as the station liked to refer to itself. The words "RIOTS GRIP JAPAN" filled the bottom third of the screen. The male newsreader's voice filled the quiet room as images of a burning Tokyo crossed the screen. "We are getting reports of a large-scale civil disturbance in the normally law-abiding country."

"Civil disturbance?!?!" Shelbi said.

"Shhh," Michael said as he leaned in toward the screen.

"We will keep an eye on the situation and bring you more developments as they warrant. Now back to our top story, from Disney princess to the queen of raunch—how did things go so wrong for America's former sweetheart?"

Michael muted the screen. "I'm glad you gave up that reporter pipe dream of yours, Kara. Those people are just an embarrassment," he said and turned his head to look at his sister. Her wheelchair was locked in place a few feet behind the couch he and Shelbi shared. Kara was unresponsive—consciousness had slipped away from her. "I'm amazed she stayed awake as long as she did." Michael stood up, walked over to Kara, and tenderly touched the hair on top of her head when he reached her.

"I have something serious to ask you," Michael said. His jaw tightened and he looked back to Shelbi, who was still seated on the couch. "You haven't been on the computer have you?"

"No!"

"Did you?"

"No!" Shelbi sternly replied. "I went in there with her." While pointing to Kara, Shelbi abruptly stopped talking.

"She's unconscious," Michael said. He was now glaring down at and towering over Shelbi.

"I went in there with her. I saw the messages from everyone maybe two seconds before you joined me in there. I swear!" Her heart beat in her chest so hard it constricted her breathing. "I swear!"

"What about Charlie?"

"What about him?"

"Anything from him?"

Shelbi knew Michael's fear had validity—the NSA had to be reviewing every communication in and out of the "hot zone" or "ground zero" or whatever they had code-named Japan by this point. But she also had a photographic memory.

"FATHER HELP ME!! THEY ATTACKED SOME R FAST ! BBLEEDING REALLY BAD ! HELP ME FATER SHOTS NOTSTOP ATTACK."

That was his last message. Nothing in that would alert the NSA to Charlie's or Michael's culpability. "SHOTS NOTSTOP ATTACK" would be read as attempted self-defense by the computer programs reading and rereading each and every text and email sent in or out of the dying nation looking for clues to the cause of the chaos.

"No, nothing. I swear, Father. Why would I lie?"

She would lie because she knew it didn't matter. That Michael would spend these precious hours worrying about nonexistent threats rather than enjoying the symphony of destruction he had wrought upon the world.

"I'm sorry," Michael said. Relief was washing over him. "I expect them to catch on pretty fast. I'm sorry, I should never have doubted you."

"It's fine." Shelbi's smile always melted Michael's heart. "I'll go refresh our drinks." She put the huge bowl of popcorn on the steel floor, picked up two half empty glasses of soda, and walked toward Michael. "You turn the real news back on, and I'll be back in here lickety-split." She pecked her lips ever so slightly against his grizzly, whiskered cheek and whispered in his ear, "Let's just relax a little. Watch your brilliance in action."

"I like the way you think," Michael said and winked at her.

"Don't worry about the US," Shelbi said confidently as she walked out of the room. "They haven't got a clue."

⋙⋘

"The BBC!" Shelbi's excitement could not be contained as she walked back into the room. Eagerly pointing to the screen that displayed the British network, she said, "Turn it up."

Michael, sitting on the couch, obeyed, and an impeccable British voice sprang to life. "Isolated incidents of the madness gripping Japan have been reported in hospitals from China to South Africa and even as close as Germany. Fears of a pandemic are growing as people are asking not if it will happen here, but when."

"I can't believe the Americans are not getting to see this."

Responding to his disappointed, childlike tone, Shelbi rubbed Michael's leg on the couch they sat on, in front of the monitors. "They can't keep up this stupidity for long. Word will seep in. Plus..." she said and looked at Michael's steel-gray eyes, and excitement twinkled in her own. "It'll mean no one here will have any chance to prepare." She kissed his cheek while trying her best to dodge the sharpest bristles of his beard.

"You are my rock," Michael said, wrapped his arm around the tiny blonde, and pressed her closer. "Without your strength I'd be nothing."

"I'll always be here for you, babe," Shelbi cooed in response. The tone of the newscaster's voice refocused the lovebirds on their program.

"We have disturbing news just coming in. It seems London has just joined the list of cities with an outbreak. Hope Tremblay joins us live from Royal London Hospital."

"Chet," the redheaded woman's voice was urgent, almost to the point of panic. "Three health care workers are confirmed deceased and an unknown number of patients are either dead or wounded in what witnesses described to me as a truly hellish scene..." A close-up of a woman's face splattered with blood appeared on the screen. Her eyes were glazed over. Microphones of varying colors and shapes pressed toward her from the bottom of the screen as she began speaking. "This Asian gentleman came in coughing up quite a storm...he...he collapsed in front of the nurse...she tried to help and...he made this sound, worse than fingernails on a chalkboard, it was so loud, and then...he...he...grabbed her...and ripped her throat out with his teeth. Others rushed to help, but I saw her get up...the nurse, that is, she bit a woman trying to help her, I ran...I don't know what happened next...I just ran."

"London shouldn't be getting this for another twenty-four hours," Michael said. He felt oddly frustrated that his plan was going ahead of schedule.

"Charlie let the gift free in the airport first," Shelbi said. Her voice was voice tinged with disgust. "Something must have happened, maybe he was spooked by security."

"Or," Michael interrupted, "a pretty girl talked to him. That usually flusters the boy." He chuckled and then said, "Whatever. It's loose, it's in the air, the fat lady is singing."

Shelbi playfully elbowed her lover and said, "Are you calling me fat?"

"Never. Besides, you have a terrible singing voice." Michael tickled his companion, who shrieked with delight.

"Hey, stop that...I want to watch TV. The end of the world doesn't have reruns." She kissed her man playfully.

"Well let's hope not." Michael smiled warmly at the woman who he could still taste on his lips. "Otherwise I've fucked up royally."

The sound of his sister coughing distracted Michael from his concubine. Kara had been repositioned toward the back of the room so he and Shelbi could have a modicum of privacy on the couch.

"Is she OK?" Shelbi asked. She felt real concern for the woman she viewed as her sister-in-law. Michael would not deal well with anything bad happening to Kara.

"She's fine."

"How long till we release her?"

"That depends on how long she wants to keep pretending she's paralyzed."

"Huh?"

"Her eyes," Michael said as if explaining something simplistic to a child. "If she were still fully paralyzed her eyes wouldn't have been darting around in her head when we were talking to her."

Kara—dressed only in a hospital gown—woke up in a new room. A single flickering light hung from the ceiling. The door in front of her was open to the steel hallway. She drew a deep breath and realized there was nothing strapped across her chest constricting her inhalation.

"I'm free." Kara thought.

She stood quickly and moved for the exit. "There it is." Across the hallway she saw the doorway that lead to freedom. It was only a few steps away and it was open.

Kara had never moved so fast in her life.

Her bare feet flew across the cold steel floor as she darted into the portal. Grabbing the first rung of the ladder, she climbed toward a round opening similar to a manhole.

She was in the shed. Shafts of light invaded the darkness through slats in the poorly constructed wall.

"The door!" Kara grabbed the rusty hinge. CLICK.

She was free.

Her feet stung as the freshly fallen snow she was running through was freezing her flesh. The pain grew with each step. It began creeping up her ankles. Her pace was slowing down.

"NO GODDAMN IT!" Panic was beginning to tighten its grasp on her. "RUN!"

The cold was becoming worse. Her legs felt numb from the knee down. Then she heard it—the sound she heard on the news from Asia. The cry was akin in tone to a baby being set on fire crossed with the noise dental tools make as they scrape and grind teeth.

Her skin and her spine reacted to the unearthly shriek as if rusty nails were being ever so slowly drawn against a blackboard. Her stomach clenched and her jaw tightened as the sound grew louder.

"Don't look back," she said as her head was turning to do just that.

It was in the doorway. The shrill sound was blaring out of its open mouth, which was filled with yellowing teeth. Its skin was the pallid gray color of death. Its blonde hair was matted and stained with what appeared to be blood.

"Oh fuck! It's Shelbi!"

Kara turned away and tried to move. Her legs were now so numb from the cold that they felt trapped—like they were in a vat of thick molasses.

"MOVE GODDAMN YOU!" Her internal commands were useless. Shelbi was closing in on her fast.

Kara looked down at her unresponsive legs. The snow was thigh deep and kept her moving at what felt like a snail's pace.

The piercing wail closing in on her filled her with a paralyzing fear—still, she fought against it and tried in vain to run.

The ghoul grabbed at Kara. The force of its grip on her upper arm was viselike. Kara turned to see the corpse. Shelbi's mouth contorted into a hungry snarl. Kara screamed as her former captor went to plunge her teeth into Kara's face...

Screaming and flailing against her leather restraints. That's when Kara, covered in a cold sweat, woke up from her dream, and back into the nightmare of her captivity.

Michael and Shelbi looked over at her, then to each other, and smiled.

Kara's heart sunk. "They saw me move."

"Sorry, but it's the only way," Michael said as he ripped off the duct tape, which had sealed his sister's lips shut. "I really apologize for the security, occasionally the antidote doesn't take."

Kara stared daggers of betrayal at her brother before snarling a single word: "Why?"

"Well, that's an open-ended question," Michael gleefully said as he stepped away from the wheelchair-bound woman. "What are you wanting to know? Why am I God? Why have I destroyed the world? Exactly which one of these 'whys' are you referring to?"

Kara's venom-filled voice snapped, "Why did you kidnap me!"

"Kidnapped?" Michael was clearly shocked by his sister's words. He knelt down in front of her, so as to look directly into her eyes. "I saved you. Haven't you been paying attention?"

Kara tried to strike out at her brother. Her arm, weak and stiff from days of bondage, barely twitched against the thick leather straps that were binding her to the wheelchair.

"Saved me?!" Kara glanced down at her body, which was secured to the wheelchair, before regaining eye contact with her brother. "This is saved?"

"Well it beats being torn limb from limb by carnivorous corpses," Shelbi said. "You could show a little appreciation for your brother saving your life."

Kara didn't acknowledge the loathsome woman's comments as she continued on with her brother. "Kidnapping me! Injecting me with God knows what! Tying me up like an animal! That's saving me?"

"Well," a confused-looking Michael replied. "In a word...yes."

"Are you completely fucking insane?!"

"Yeah, that's it!" Fury suddenly erupted from Michael like lava exploding from a volcano. "I'm the fucking crazy one!"

"Honey," Shelbi said—her voice was loving and nervous as she interjected. "Let's just breathe, OK?"

"Shut up!" Michael snapped at the small blonde before continuing his rant. "Think I'm crazy, Kara? Huh?" His wild eyes were fueled by a cocktail of rage and Shelbi's homemade medications.

"I'm not crazy, Kara. I'm God!"

"You're not fucking God! Let me go you fucking idiot. NOW!"

Michael's face broke out in a wide grin. "I'm not God yet, but I will be soon."

"You're fucking crazy. Let me go!"

Ignoring his sister's plea, Michael continued: "Everyone always thought God created man, but it's the other way around." Michael began to circle his sister as he talked. "You see it's a simple quantum fact, if enough people believe in something they can manifest it. Humans created Gods to help them cope."

"So your big plan is to become a make-believe God? Are you listening to yourself?"

"No, all the Gods—every one of them since the dawn of mankind—were, and are, absolutely real. It's just that people created them through their love and belief, not the other way around."

"Uh huh. Please untie me."

"I am going to kill every person on this planet that believes in every God other than me. My followers who went forth from here two by two shall rebuild this world in my image. Their devotion and love shall elevate me into a deity. The only deity. Michael the Father, the one and only true God."

"You aren't God!"

"You are starting to sound like a parrot." Michael flapped his arms like a bird and squawked out, "You're not God WAAA Kara want a cracker WAAAA." He stopped in front of her, grasped her leather-bound arms, stared into her eyes, and continued: "My followers are going to be the only survivors of my plague. They will find one another and then, united by a common language, religion, and race, they will form a new paradigm of peace and love with me as its one and only true God."

"United in race?" Kara scoffs. "Is racism a side effect of psychosis?"

"I'm not a racist. I'm pragmatic. I'm trying to reset the whole world. Why would I throw in extra variables that could muck everything up? Religion and race: the two great killing excuses for mankind. If everyone is the same color it's just safer."

"Great, you're a crazy racist who lives in a compound in the woods. Fuckin' great."

Michael began circling her again and ignored her insults. "My original followers will be immune to the plague but their offspring will not."

"Sounds brilliant, zombie babies." Kara's eyes burned at her brother. "Your new world order won't last very long."

"Ugh!" Michael, exasperated, walked over to a bookshelf, withdrew a thick tome, and turned to his bound sister. "This is the book of Michael."

"Ha!" Kara exploded in laughter at her brother. "Oh my god that's fuckin' hilarious."

He opened the book up and faced her so she could see the contents.

"Oh great," she responded while still snickering. "It's in gibberish." The pages in front of her were a series of unintelligible symbols.

"No, it's in English," Michael replied. "I just replaced the traditional English alphabet with symbols of my own. I don't want our ancestors being able to read any language except mine. You see in my religion the apocalypse comes first. Killing off the wicked and leaving only the pure behind to start over again."

"You're not a God."

"My original flock will be immune to my little zombie plague, however, their offspring will not. The book of Michael has religious ceremonies dealing with the disposal of flesh without soul, assuring the living that this is a sign from their God...me...that once someone dies and the corpse rises. It proves beyond a shadow of a doubt that the soul of their loved one is now pure and in Heaven next to me, their loving Father. The flesh, the repository of all sin, is then destroyed and discarded." Michael smiles. "See, it makes perfect sense."

"Sounds retarded to me." Kara sneers at her brother.

"You are obviously still feeling the side effects of the inoculations." Michael's voice was dripping with sarcasm as he mocked his sister. "Sometimes it takes a while for the neural pathways to fully reconnect after the initial fungal infection. You do remember me…I am your brother Michael."

"I know who you are, Michael," Kara's venom-laced voice replied. "So where is our sister? Did you decide to kidnap her, too? Or were you too much of a pussy to go after her?"

"I assume Jane's on her way here. No doubt to save us and the world," Michael responded.

"And," Shelbi piped in, feeling that it was finally safe to speak, "when she gets here, we are going to need you to help us."

"With what?" Kara shot back.

"My dear sister," Michael said. "We need you to convince her that the only way out of this is to join us and let me inoculate her."

"Yeah," Kara sneered. "Like that is going to happen."

⊰⊱

The sky surrounding Yokota Air Base outside Tokyo was engulfed in smoke from the inferno surrounding the US military installation. Another fire burning in the center of the base choked the air with the smell of burning human flesh. "Every last one!" the silver-haired Lieutenant Commander Jane Kerr snapped at her men as they added bodies to the fire. "I want no chance of those fucking things coming back again. Watch them until they're ash." The dead soldiers' bodies sizzled and cracked as they were unceremoniously heaved onto the pyramid-shaped funeral pyre.

"Genevieve! Update," Kerr barked into a communicator.

"Fire is holding them back ma'am," Sergeant April Genevieve replied, sitting in front of a bank of monitors located deep in the bowels of the base. She watched the footage from the drones she controlled. Flickering screens showed the base surrounded by a wall of flame, holding millions of screaming dead at bay.

"Roger," Kerr acknowledged. "How many did we lose? Over."

Sergeant Genevieve looked to one monitor on the bottom right of the wall. The feed from this drone showed infrared imagery of the base. Genevieve read the number flashing in the corner of the screen.

"Computer is counting eight hundred sixty-three living targets still within base, ma'am."

"Three percent of us left," Kerr thought. Her mind was as fast as her body was strong—it easily calculated the percentage of survivors from the twenty-five thousand stationed at Yokota.

"Roger that. What's the status with communications?"

"Emergency communication has just been reestablished," Sergeant Genevieve said calmly while her fingers furiously attacked a keyboard. "Trying to raise DC as we speak."

"Roger," Kerr replied as she looked out at the carnage from days of fighting. "Un-fucking real," she thought as she surveyed the base turned battlefield. The smoke from the conflagration surrounding the military outpost choked out all sunlight. The only illumination came from the flames devouring the world outside the base's breached gates, which made the landscape even more hellish in appearance. Silhouettes of soldiers with weapons at the ready stalked the battlefield, scouring the combat zone for any sign of movement from the corpses littering the ground.

"Ma'am I have link to DC established. I have a priority message from Washington," Sergeant Genevieve said.

"Route it to my HUD," Kerr said, referring to the Heads Up Display. A video popped up in her goggles, which flashed the words "PRIORITY ALPHA."

A grainy image of General Jim Hermitage, head of the NSA, appeared in Kerr's HUD and said, "Jane! Are you OK?" The frantic voice of the General, a man she had known for years, stiffened her spine.

"I am fine, sir. Yokota Air Base is secure and operational." Unlike her desk jockey former lover on the other end of the line,

Lieutenant Commander Jane Kerr wasn't about to break protocol just because things were getting ugly.

"The president is dead." The words slapped Kerr across the face hard.

"Vice president, too. The bunker went bad." Hermitage, sitting alone in a room filled with computers, looked away from the screen. Behind him, three bodies lay, bullet holes gaping from their skulls. The six-inch-thick steel blast door was locked. A single monitor on the wall next to the portal showed the monsters clawing at the secured entrance.

"Who's in command?"

"I am Jane." He turned away from the hallway feed. The former political and military leaders' corpses were breaking limbs as they pummeled the door looking for food. "Everyone else is dead."

Hermitage's eyes burned brightly as he stared at his old friend and occasional lover. "Take the Aurora VII," he said, referring to the secret transport jet capable of Mach 8 that was used to bring special ops anywhere in the world. "You are being assigned to secure Barnes Air National Guard Base. Find your family. Keep them safe."

"Sir?"

"No questions. And drop the sir bullshit. There's no one else listening anymore."

"Jim, we held them back. We can win this thing." She hated the despair and desperation in his voice. "We can."

"You can. That's your job." Hermitage tried to smile, but his face just grimaced. "We found a weakness in the virus. Radiation stops the infection."

"How?"

"Not sure, but surveillance footage clearly shows Fukushima prefecture had no outbreak. The entire country erupted in this plague except there."

Jane knew this man better than she knew anyone. With a wary voice, she asked, "What are you planning?"

"I've run the numbers again and again. In twenty-four hours the coasts will be overrun. Using NSA protocols I've remotely shut down every nuclear plant on the continent. Hopefully that will stop further infection. The tsunamis will scrub the coasts clean."

"Tsunamis?"

"In twenty-four hours everything we have will be launched at the ice caps."

"What!" Jane couldn't believe what she was hearing.

"The whole arsenal. Every nuke we have will be launched. The populations near the coasts can't be saved. So we are going to wash them out to sea."

"Sir?"

"I said drop the sir bullshit! This was no snap decision, Jane. We are trying to salvage what we can. We lost, Jane. We lost."

"Sir." Jane's tone was terse. "We have not lost."

Ignoring her declaration, Hermitage continued: "The CDC computers project we will lose the coasts within twenty-four hours. The nuclear strike on Greenland alone will cause a massive tsunami to scrub the East Coast of the infected. Inland the infection has been spreading slower—those communities might stand a fighting chance at controlling the remaining infected."

"Sir. Tsunamis can push debris hundreds of miles inland." Jane's voice was cold, calculating, and professional. "If the wave pushes these zombies inland, won't this be throwing gasoline on a fire?"

"We have run simulation after simulation," Hermitage replied. "The debris field combined with the velocity of the water should rip them to shreds."

"Jim."

"Jane, I am sending you the evacuation plan for your area. Modify it as you see fit. Sea levels will rise approximately two hundred feet within six hours of the strike."

"Don't do this Jim!"

"It's our only chance."

"You are going to irradiate the whole world. Everyone will be dead from cancer."

"I'd rather take my chances fighting tumors. That fight is winnable."

"WE HELD THEM BACK IN TOKYO!" Jane yelled. "GODDAMN IT, JIM! WE HELD THEM BACK!"

"Uh huh, you did. But within twelve hours there will be nothing to burn around the base. After that you would have had enough ammo to last what...five, maybe six hours...then what?"

"I'd figure it out."

"You'd die, Jane! You, and your men would die." Exasperated, the general continued: "I don't have time for another plan. The nukes launch tomorrow. You should feel lucky, Jane."

"Really."

"Yeah. The computer projects Massachusetts to have a lower infection rate than almost anywhere. Guess having all that practice staying off the streets during snowstorms and terrorist manhunts paid off. It's the only state that pretty much shuttered up and shut down at the first sign of infection."

"Jim."

"Don't, Jane. We are both professionals. We will both make it out of this. I'm sending you access codes for communication overrides. Besides your area there are fifteen evacuation zones across the continent. I expect you to secure your area first. Once you do, go save the rest of them. And if you could rescue my sorry ass, I'd be appreciative." Jim cracked a smile. "It's what you do after all. I'll see you in a few days"

The screen went black.

"Fuck!!!" Jane stared at the black square in her HUD.

"This is Lieutenant Commander Kerr. Get the Aurora ready. We are bugging out."

⟞⟝ ⟞⟝

"You want me to help you?" Kara was stunned at the audacity of her brother.

"Yes, we don't want to hurt her," Shelbi said.

"You mean you don't want her to hurt you."

"That, too," Michael responded. "She can be a little, shall we say, intense." While he was growing up, Michael's much older sister Jane was a stranger to him. She was already in the military when Michael was barely out of diapers and with the exception of the occasional holiday when she would come home on leave, he never saw her. To a sociopath like Michael if you didn't serve a purpose he had no use for you. Jane served no purpose as far as Michael could tell.

"How about you undo these straps, and I'll think about it." Kara was utterly stunned when Shelbi leaned over and began to unbuckle the thick leather constraints.

"Absolutely," Michael said. His head was reeling as Shelbi's homemade drugs coursed through his bloodstream. "You are still going to be weak, probably be another day before you can walk."

"Wait until you see how far the gift has spread," Shelbi said. She was as enthusiastic as a small child on Christmas morning. "You won't believe it. Wait till you see the TV."

The first strap came off. Her right arm no longer held down, Kara's first response was to break Shelbi's nose. Her arm, however, didn't respond. It lifted only a few inches off the armrest before limply falling back down. "That was amazing," Shelbi said after seeing the movement. "Did you see that, honey? She is really recovering fast."

"Not fast enough," Kara thought, disappointed that Shelbi's nose wasn't splayed open with blood gushing from it.

"She might even be able to walk in a few hours."

"That's great." Michael's smile hid his concern. He would have preferred her recovery come after everyone outside of his bunker was dead.

Things were moving too fast for Michael.

The gift was appearing far ahead of schedule, manifesting in small outbreaks worldwide, and while it was good to know how viciously infectious it was, it also gave populations time to prepare. This worried Michael. Countries all over the globe had begun mobilizing their militaries. Armed police dressed in riot gear and full gas masks were a common sight at hospitals everywhere. Air travel was shut down. The United States had set up military roadblocks to stop interstate travel on the highways, except for food and medical supplies. But what really concerned Michael was the reaction of the world's populace.

He expected terror in the streets. He wanted panic. He hoped for raping and pillaging. These soulless miscreants he infected would surely act in the most heinous way possible to try to save themselves. That wasn't happening.

Instead of panic, stoicism seemed to settle on the world's populations. Areas where small outbreaks were contained became worldwide beacons of hope. Stories had filled the news of people acting heroically: the London nurse who used herself as bait while the hospital staff evacuated the maternity ward; the Oklahoma City firemen who used hoses to pin the infected inside Community Hospital.

Shelbi told Michael not to worry. That the stories were just civilization's version of pissing in the win—after all, infectious diseases aren't affected by such nonsense as hope or optimism. While Michael knew she was right, it still infuriated him that humanity was trying to fight back instead of simply cowering in fear until their inevitable and violent demise.

Michael knew that when Kara saw these stories, she would try to escape—both she and Shelbi were inoculated against the infection, and blood from either woman could be used to mass-produce a vaccine. The last thing he needed was his sister fully recovered while there was still a possibility of stopping his plague.

Shelbi freed Kara's left arm and asked, "Can you move it?" Kara's left arm repeated her right's weak movement before also falling limp on the armrest. "Oh, trust me, Shelbi, I'm trying," Kara replied through gritted teeth.

"If I have Shelbi refasten her straps, I'll never get her to willingly join us," Michael thought as his concubine methodically freed his sibling from her bonds. "Realistically she can't escape. The entrance is locked—she won't be able to walk for hours much less run or put up a fight. Let her think you trust her."

"This is going to be great," Shelbi gushed as she unfastened the strap that had immobilized Kara's head against the high-backed wheelchair. "The two of us raising kids together, repopulating the world."

"Excuse me!" Kara was stunned. "Kids! Did you say raising kids?"

"Yes, me raising Michael's children, and you raising all the others."

"We haven't told her that part yet, darling." Michael was annoyed. Shelbi's enthusiasm had once again enabled her to put her foot squarely in her mouth.

"Oops." She smiled. "But really, you have to tell her sometime, might as well be now."

"Tell me what!"

"Michael has sperm samples from all our followers. He'll artificially inseminate you once the danger is over and we begin rebuilding the world." While looking at Kara's disgusted expression, Shelbi added, "Oh my you didn't think Michael would...oh God no! Incest would be totally counterproductive. We don't need a

53

new world filled with hemophiliacs or, as you fondly call them, re-tards." Shelbi patted Kara's head. "That would be stupid. You can be so silly, sister."

"Yeah, that's me. Jumping to crazy conclusions just because my brother kidnapped me, strapped me in a wheelchair, put me inside a doomsday bunker, dumped snakes on me, killed four men with his bare hands, and set loose a bioweapon that's destroying the world. I sure am silly to think he would harm me in any way."

"That's the spirit." Sarcasm always eluded Shelbi, especially when she was so heavily medicated. "Originally you were going to have all the men as a harem." Nudging Kara's arm, she leaned in and said, "Being God's sister has its perks." Kara felt vomit creep up to the top of her neck before oozing back down her gullet as the deranged woman spoke. "But they had to question your broth-er, my lover, our God. And now they're all dead. But lucky for us we have plenty of DNA samples, so we'll be good."

"Why don't you just tell her where the exit is?" Michael asked. He was clearly frustrated at his woman's exuberance.

"OK. It's..."

"NO!" Michael shouted and then said with as much calm as he could muster, "I was joking."

"Oh, OK. No reason to yell." Shelbi smiled at her man.

Michael looked to his sister and said, "I would never force some-thing on you against your will."

Kara responded by looking down at where the leather straps had cut into the skin of her forearms, then looked back at her brother. With sarcasm oozing from her voice, she said, "Nice to know."

"Great!" Michael said. He felt a shower of relief wash over him knowing that Kara believed him. Shelbi jumped up and down while squealing, "This is awesome, we are finally a family!"

"Oh my fucking God! They really are fucking insane!" The thought hit Kara with the force of a freight train. Her brother couldn't understand she wasn't serious? He really thought everything was OK? As she watched her two captors embrace and kiss, she felt true despair. "He's really completely out of his mind." Her two captors, still locked in a tight embrace, began slowly rocking back and forth while Shelbi hummed "Michael, Row Your Boat Ashore."

"These two are out of their minds." The thought was so obvious. Kara was ashamed at how long it had taken her to realize the truth of her situation. "This...all of this...this is has to be...complete bullshit."

⟨——⟩

Kara's fuzzy thoughts recalled the television footage of the carnage. "No way," she thought. "Impossible." She reassured herself. "This is some brainwashing gambit they are playing." The thought that her brother had kidnapped her to brainwash her into joining his cult, while not comforting, still made more sense than the idea that her little brother had invented a zombie virus that was destroying civilization.

"If he built a bunker, he could easily fake some newscasts." She looked back toward the couple. "I haven't been awake very much. I haven't even seen much footage." A sharp pain hit her chest, where she was injected. "I don't even know what I was shot with." She struggled with and then abandoned an attempt to lift her hand to the wound. "He could've given me anything. That was probably a Japanese horror movie he showed me while I was tripping."

"C'mon, Kara, let's get real here. There's no virus." Closing her eyes, Kara thought: "You've been kidnapped and given drugs. He's trying to brainwash you into joining his cult." An odd sense of relief mixed with sorrow cascaded over her as she gave in to logic. "Just gain his trust—he's so far gone that it shouldn't be a problem." After opening her eyes, she saw the two still slowly rocking back and forth by the glow of the monitors. "Just take my time, there's no rush. There's no apocalypse." Kara wasn't sure how long she had been unconscious. "Tommy will realize when I don't come back to work something's wrong." She felt hope growing in her "By the time I figure out how to escape, this area will probably be crawling with search teams." Kara smiled for the first time since her ordeal started. She felt there was finally a light at the end of this tunnel.

"Look," Shelbi delicately whispered in Michael's ear. "She's smiling."

Michael saw his sister's expression and her smile filled him with joy. "She believes," he whispered back to the blonde embracing him. "That means the hard part is finally over."

"Would it be OK..." Shelbi hesitantly asked, "to read to her?"

"I think," Michael responded, "that's a great idea."

≈╪ ╪≈

"For Michael saw that the flesh was wicked and distracted mankind from their duty." Shelbi's tone was reverential as she read from the book of Michael. "Severing the spirit from the flesh He showed man the folly of earthly distractions. For once the soul departs to join Father in Heaven, the flesh—afraid of true death—struggles on." Shelbi sniffled and then wiped a small tear from her eye. "Unencumbered by a soul, the flesh reverts to its most base behavior. Survival at all costs."

Peering up from the leather-bound tome in her hand, Shelbi peeked to see how Kara was reacting to her brother's brilliant words before continuing on. "For while the soul is pure the flesh is wicked. The soul concerns itself with love, charity, and compassion. The flesh cares only about greed. What it wants, what it needs. Unconcerned for the world around it. It battles the soul's higher yearnings for its own base pleasures." Shelbi delicately turned the

56

vellum page and continued: "When the dead rise as flesh without soul they show the living the senselessness of earthly delights. It is the desire of the flesh from which all evil springs. For, know this my children, that as evil as the flesh is, it compares little to how truly beautiful and pure your soul will be once it joins with Father in the afterlife. Thus is the blessing of the undead, for they instruct us to look past our greedy, small lives and to concentrate on truth, love, kindness, and generosity, those works that bring pleasure to our Father. Michael, hallowed be his name, His kingdom comes, when your flesh is done, your soul brought into Heaven, Take not your daily bread until all the poor have been fed. Only this shall deliver you from the wrath of the dead and the punishment of your Father, who art in Heaven...amen."

"Well that was fuckin' creepy as hell," Kara thought as she sat across from Shelbi in Michael's cold room.

"That's...really inspirational." Kara said out loud. "Thank you for that reading."

"Can't you just feel Michael's love jumping off the page and into your heart?" Shelbi asked and placed her right hand on her chest as if pledging allegiance. "Your brother so loves the world that he's killing it, in order to save it."

"Like I said, truly awe inspiring."

While grinning from ear to ear. Shelbi carefully closed the holy book and placed it on the table separating the two women. "The end of the sinful world is so close now. It's truly inevitable."

"Uh huh." Kara agreeably nodded, still amazed by the depths of the insanity spewed forth by both her captors. "I have to apologize and give Jaden a raise as soon as I am out of here," she thought to herself.

"I could read more if you like," Shelbi said. Her enthusiasm seemed to be growing by the second.

"No, no," Kara responded. "I think three hours with the good book is plenty for now."

"Are you sure?" Shelbi asked.

Kara's audible response was: "Yes...umm...I am so filled with love, I need time to digest it all." Her internal response was: "Biggest fuckin' raise I can afford. Maybe I'll get Jaden a company car."

⇒⊹ ⊹⇐

The Aurora scorched the atmosphere as its plasma engines thrust into overdrive. Sunlight glinted off its shiny radar-eluding surface, giving the huge triangular aircraft an otherworldly appearance befitting a Hollywood fantasy rather than a harsh military reality.

The inside of the Aurora, however, looked as mundane as every other military aircraft. Dark-gray metal interior. Dim lighting. Astonishingly uncomfortable seating. US military through and through.

"Here's the deal, ladies." Jane always addressed her squad as such. "They want us to protect this airbase." She pressed a button on a gauntlet and a map appeared inside each team member's HUD, highlighting the location of the Barnes Air National Guard Base in Westfield.

"Our leaders have decided to launch nukes at the ice caps, believing the tsunamis will wash the dead out to sea." During Jane's speech, the map displayed a much broader view encompassing three states: Massachusetts, Connecticut, and Rhode Island, all outlined in red. The image animated to show the projected sea level rise. "This is what will happen to the coasts." Her men watched as Connecticut and Rhode Island both submerged completely save for some hills. Half of Massachusetts—from the eastern coast to the Worcester Hills in the state's middle—became completely submerged. "As you can see, once Connecticut sinks, the new coastline will be here." She pointed to Westfield, which was half-submerged in the simulation—the airbase had barely escaped the projected flood. "These are the refugee camp locations in the Berkshires."

She highlighted several areas in the Berkshire Mountains. "The army corps of engineers are arriving now and are preparing those camps."

"We are going to be here, ladies." She highlighted a T intersection next to the Westfield River. "This is where we are going to act as bait and fuck all those things up while everyone evacuates."

"Ma'am, isn't this tsunami going to wash those things right up on our doorsteps?"

"The boys in DC assure me that won't happen, so I fully expect them to be wrong and leave us up to our assholes in hungry corpses. There's no way we can stop that launch. If we could that's where we'd be heading. This is the shit sandwich we've been served, ladies. We've got to deal with it."

"How are we securing the base by being bait?" one soldier asked.

"We are going to use fire to corral them and funnel them right to us. Away from the base and the refugees."

Thermopylae. The soldier replied, referring to the ancient Greek battle.

"Exactly. Study up the topography, ladies. This place is my hometown. By the time we are off this bird I want you to know Westfield better than I do. The brains in DC think radiation kills this disease, because of this info," Jane said and pressed a button on a small keypad that was sown into the sleeve of her uniform. "Which I'm downloading to all your HUDs. As you will learn, it looks like the radiation stops spontaneous transformation in these things, however, we don't know how much radiation or how much exposure time is needed to actually kill the virus. There is no evidence to suggest these creatures, once transformed, are affected by the radiation. They are still venomous. If they bite you, you will turn. Just like before. We know how fast shit spirals out of control. It still can. And probably will until the radiation takes hold. All six nuclear plants in New England are already in meltdown, so we have that going for us." Her lips cracked a sarcastic smile. "Do your homework. Learn this place inside and out. I have a speech to prepare for the locals."

⇥ ⇤

"Could I ask you a question, Shelbi?" Kara asked.

"Of course, sister," Shelbi said and smiled, feeling that Kara was truly becoming a believer. "Anything."

"I'm sorry," Kara replied. "Everything was so fuzzy earlier, but did you say Michael wasn't injected with the cure?"

"Oh yes, quite true, God cannot be incapacitated in front of his disciples." Shelbi was brimming with love for her sister. "We decided that at the first sign of infection we would inoculate, but that probably wouldn't be until after we emerged from the temple complex."

"Temple complex?" Kara thought. "I would have gone with Dr. Mengele's fallout shelter."

Kara said, "That makes sense. But wouldn't it be safer to vaccinate him now? After all it's just us here now. No followers left to impress." Kara knew Shelbi would say no. There was no way any of this could be real, so she knew Michael's stupid little girlfriend would bend logic to fit the story they were feeding her. After three hours of Shelbi reading Michael's deranged ramblings about his deity status, Kara was convinced that this was all an elaborate brainwashing attempt by the duo. "I love my brother more than anything I want him to be safe from this plague." Kara waited for Shelbi to lie to her.

"I love him, too," Shelbi said as she reached her hands to tenderly grasp Kara's. "I love him so much you…well, you know and I know you're right, but try to convince him of that." She rolled her eyes and said, "Gods don't like being questioned."

Kara nodded—it was the easiest way to look agreeable while swallowing the small amount of vomit that rose to her throat when Shelbi touched her.

"I pledge to you, sister, that I will never let anything happen to him," Shelbi said. She felt so touched at this moment of deep and real bonding with her sister.

"I know." Kara smiled at the stupid girl she was slowly sizing up. "Could you help me up?" Hours of Book-of-Michael thumping had given her body time to regain strength. Unfortunately, at the moment that strength had only risen to the level of an eighty-year-old woman.

"Absolutely," Shelbi stood and lent her arm for support. "You are making great progress."

"Thanks. So when does the world come to an end?"

"Well, it already ended for most of Asia. China was decimated. Apparently the heavy pollution there lowered the immune systems of the population so much that it spread like wildfire. Way ahead of schedule. As for everywhere else, most urban centers, which are almost always on the coasts, should go first. Rural areas could hold out for a few weeks, until the swarms descend on them."

"Swarms?" Kara asked.

"Yes, the fungus, although individually infecting its prey, is still a single organism."

"I'm not following."

"The fungus releases chemical signals that instruct the hordes to sweep through areas in search of prey. They swarm. The infection is really just a numbers game. Kill enough up front, build up the swarm, and the annihilation of anyone left uninfected is inevitable. One hundred percent. I ran the numbers myself. They will move from the coasts and kill their way inland."

"I'm not following. How is that a single organism?"

"Sorry, each infected person essentially becomes a single cell in a much larger entity. When you watch them move from above on the TV box it's evident. The fungus, I theorize, uses chemical signals that coordinate the infected to act as one, like a school of fish or a flock of birds."

"Michael seemed..." Kara paused as she chose her words carefully, "...perplexed by the fast ones. Why?"

"The fast ones bother him. They don't make sense, as there is no equivalent in nature. I believe it's simply the level of infection in the subjects. Michael, big surprise here, won't commit to my idea."

"He is stubborn like that."

"You're telling me sister."

Kara nodded, swallowed, and smiled.

"He thinks there's another variable at play which we haven't accounted for." Shelbi rolled her eyes. "He is such a worrywart. I mean, whatever the fast ones are, they are going to decompose and fall apart just like the rest of them in a few weeks."

"Then the faithful emerge from their strongholds and restore harmony to all things living," Kara said, looking to cement her burgeoning bond with the lunatic blonde.

Tears of joy streamed down Shelbi's cheeks. Kara knew she had Shelbi's trust. But more importantly she knew she now had the upper hand on her captor.

"Lieutenant commander." The pilot's voice sounded tired as he tried to contact the new boss. "Lieutenant commander Kerr, do you read me? Over."

"Loud and clear." Jane's voice sounded distant. Three hours on the Aurora to the Greylock airbase in the Adirondacks, the only runway long enough to land an Aurora on the East Coast, had given her plenty of time to analyze the plan Jim had sent her. The flight from Upstate New York on the Chinook helicopter to Westfield gave her the time to drastically change the plan so that it might work. Physically she was less than fifty feet behind the pilot in the dual-bladed helicopter, Mentally she had been time traveling.

"We are less than fifteen minutes outside of Barnes." The airbase in Westfield was home to the 104th Fighter Wing, whose fearsome fleet of F-15s had been patrolling the Northeast skies for years. These were the people assigned to prevent another 9/11. These were some of the people she would soon command.

"Roger," she responded to the pilot.

She was approaching home for the first time in years. Memories from this New England town flooded her as she flew overhead: the Fourth of July fireworks at Stanley Park; that time when her kid sister Kara somehow got her hair caught in the spokes of that fat kid Tommy's bicycle. That warm September morning walking her baby brother to Abner Gibbs Elementary School for his first day of kindergarten. Seeing the bruises he had on his thighs later that same day as he whooshed down a Slip'N Slide in their backyard during that humid afternoon.

"Daddy says bruises means he loves me," the cherub said when questioned by his sister. That memory still made her blood boil.

Flying over Pine Hill Cemetery, remembering the look of fear on her stepfather's face as he took his last breath. That memory grounded her. It was the first time she had killed someone so intimately.

"Glad he suffered." That feeling of satisfaction knowing she saved her family from that monster. It only took 15 minutes of 'enhanced interrogation' before he confessed to molesting Michael. Jane tortured him for three more hours until he finally died. The car accident she staged to cover the murder was impeccable. The authorities never caught on.

The church in the town square, rebuilt in the 1700s after a fire and still the tallest structure in the city, was now visible from the chopper. Jane took a deep breath.

His death never came up in her nightmares, like so many of the others did.

The chopper banked to the left, toward Barnes. Kerr's memories turned a dark corner, and she was reminded of the funeral.

That look of utter despair and devastation on little Michael's round face. Never in the history of the world had someone been so distraught at having their life saved.

"He didn't understand. He was just a kid."

Her mom's face as they lowered the casket into the ground. She had just lost the second man she loved, and the last one she ever would. Remaining alone until the cancer took her, she never remarried. Jane could still see her dead eyes. No longer willing or able to endure the pain of loss. Killing that bastard tore her family apart. Michael and her mother were never the same toward her after the funeral.

They never confronted her, but she could see when her mom would look at her, she knew. From then on her mother would barely address or acknowledge her firstborn.

Jane saved her brother, only to lose her mother.

Kara was different. Kara understood.

At the funeral, as their mom led Kara to the minivan, she looked back to her sister and mouthed the words "thank you."

They never spoke of it again.

That memory, of her baby sister, was what Jane always thought of before battle. Jane knew she was put on this earth to protect the innocent. It drove her. It focused her. It was her touchstone. And it was cracking.

"Where are you two?"

Jane had been trying to find her family since she was ordered to abandon Japan.

The pizza place said they were on a trip, but the NSA database showed no sign of them on any passenger manifests.

"Did the plague already get to them?" The thought nipped at her brain as the helicopter streaked above the skies of Westfield. "No, it couldn't have. They are alive...I can feel it."

━┤+ +┝━

Strength.

With each hour that passed more and more of it flowed through Kara's frame. She could now walk unassisted, although never unattended.

Shelbi had returned to reading out loud from the book of Michael—Kara half-listened as she walked about Michael's room. Shelbi thought this was great. Her sister-in-law was gaining both strength of body, and through scripture, strength of spirit.

Kara studied the room. Her sister had always taught her, "If you are in a bad spot, look for anything that could be used as a weapon." She didn't plan on using weapons to escape, for that she was going to rely on cunning. But it was good to be prepared just in case.

Thwap.

Shelbi closed the holy book and said, "The brilliance of it is impeccable."

"Yeah totally," Kara replied as she pondered the lethality of each item in the room.

"I can't get over it," Shelbi said. "It's almost over. The world is literally in its death throes."

"What's in that?" Kara asked her captor while pointing to a silver container approximately the size of a thermos.

"The gift," Shelbi replied, "and the antidote."

"May I?" Kara asked while reaching her hand out toward the very solid-looking metal cylinder.

"Sure. Just be careful."

"I will." The object felt heavy to Kara, around five or six pounds. Fairly hefty for something six inches high by three inches around. "This works," she thought. "Real solid."

Kara looked over to Shelbi and said, "Can I open it? I'd like to see what it looks like."

"It's not much to look at," Shelbi replied. "Those are just the hypodermics filled with it. Keeping it in the dark lets the fungi metabolize at optimum performance."

"So may I look?"

"Sure, just not too long. Take a quick peek then seal it back up. If you want, I could get one of the mushrooms from the farm for you."

"You have a farm down here?" Kara asked as she unscrewed the top half of the shiny cylinder from the bottom, revealing the six syringes contained within. Plunger side up, their thick needles were attached but inserted into black Styrofoam for safety.

"Yes, it takes quite a bit from the volva to produce the antidote."

"Excuse me?" Kara chuckled with a smile as she was reattaching the top of the metal container. "Where do you get the antidote from?"

"Ugh!" Shelbi thought. "Why can't she be as smart as her brother?" Smart people, in Shelbi's opinion, were far easier to manipulate.

"The volva is the mycological term for the macrofeature left behind by the peridium that encloses the immature fruit bodies of the cordycep fungi," Shelbi replied, talking in a slightly slower pace, as if instructing a child. She paused slightly and continued: "Not to be confused with the pileus that forms on the top of most agarics, more commonly known as the cap."

"Really?" Kara asked. "I'd love to see one."

"So you understood that?" Shelbi's expression seemed slightly confused to Kara.

"Yes, absolutely." Kara had worked the line at her restaurant for over a decade. Having a sharp, almost photographic memory was necessary if you wanted to get orders barked out by waitresses over the din of a professional kitchen right. "The volva, the mycological term for the macrofeature left behind by the peridium which encloses the immature fruit bodies of the cordicep fungi."

"Wow, you pick up stuff fast." Shelbi knew Kara was lying. There was no way she understood the words she parroted so perfectly. In Shelbi's opinion she simply wasn't smart enough.

"Thank you," Kara said in the most sisterly tone she could stomach.

"I'll go get one out from the farm," Shelbi said in the most friendly tone she could fake.

"Great! I'll be right here," Kara said smiled.

"I know," Shelbi replied as she walked out the door. Shutting it behind her, she quietly locked the door.

⚔⚔

"She lied to me." Shelbi's words were hushed as she spoke to Michael in the communication center.

Michael didn't avert his eyes from the wall of monitors he was scrutinizing as he replied. Seduced by the stream of carnage in front of him, he managed a distracted-sounding "about what?"

"Her comprehension of mycology," Shelbi said

"Are you listening to yourself?" Michael asked as he turned toward her, his charming grin enhancing his steel-gray eyes. "Come here, baby." Michael patted the couch cushion next to him. "Stress is getting to you."

Shelbi hated when he would do that. Just brush off her worries and concerns like she was a scared child. She also hated that he had always been right. "She pretended to comprehend basic biological definitions! She doesn't even know the difference between a volva and a vulva!"

"Does she know what a Volvo is?" Michael asked and winked.

"That's not funny, Michael!" Shelbi snarled.

"They are boxy but they are safe."

"MICHAEL!"

"Seriously, baby." He knew how to diffuse these little tense moments in their relationship. "You probably intimidated her when you started talking about the gift. That is how the conversation got around to mycology, or am I way off base here?"

Shelbi knew deep down Michael was right. It didn't piss her off any less. If anything, the passive-aggressive way Michael just seemed to put her down for being smarter than his sister really upset her. But she knew the safest thing to do was swallow her pride and give up before the man she loved lost his temper with her. "You're right, I'm being silly," she replied.

"Good," Michael said. "Come here, let's watch the greatest show ever."

"OK, but I'm supposed to bring back a mushroom from the farm for Kara."

"She can wait. How's her recovery?"

"Pretty good. She should be good as new in a couple of hours," Shelbi said as she joined her lover on the couch. "How's the gift-giving going this holiday season?"

"I'm worried about the fast ones."

"Seriously baby, you worry way too much."

"There is no reason for this behavior." Michael was worried, very worried. His plan had been impeccable, and it was almost unfolding that way. But the fast ones, they weren't supposed to have happened. He was especially worried that the disciples he had sent forth two by two to rebuild a better world would not be prepared for this unforeseen danger. Michael, however, did not want to worry his woman with his actual fears.

"It's probably the infection level is higher in some individuals. But honestly, what does it matter? They are still corpses. Fast or slow they will still rot away in a few weeks." Shelbi's logic probably would have put Michael at ease had it not been for a most unexpected sound suddenly filling the bunker.

NEE-uuu. NEE-uu. The alarm sounded out, alerting the two that the motion-detecting sensor at the end of the dirt road had just been tripped.

Michael clicked a blue button on his remote control. The image of three Massachusetts State Police vehicles approaching his abode replaced the news carnage on the screens.

"Still think I worry too much?" Michael asked.

Shelbi said nothing.

⊶ ⊷

When Lieutenant Commander Kerr landed at the base of the 104th Fighter Wing, Homeland Security protocol XV-1 was initiated. Also known as martial law, the protocol put the hometown native in charge of everything within her designated area of operations. Her first order upon taking charge was to send the assets located closest to her sister's and her brother's homes to search for them.

"Notify command we are approaching target," the voice of a state trooper squawked out over Michael's police scanner.

"Roger."

"You were right! They are looking for her!" Shelbi was astounded, yet again, by her lover's ability to predict his enemies' moves. "But where's your sister Jane? You said she'd be the one breaking down the door to find you and Kara."

"Shhh!" Michael wanted quiet as his mind raced over details. The alarm had been shut off. Kara was safely locked in. The hatch to the temple complex was secured and concealed. Michael took out his phone and quickly punched in several codes. "OK, it's armed," he said.

Michael had put surveillance cameras around the woods surrounding his cabin. Paranoid and maniacal by nature, he feared that one day the powers that be might find out what he was up to and launch a Ruby Ridge–style ambush on him. He had thought, considering the current crisis, that his defensive systems would wind up never being used. He didn't like being wrong, but he did like the idea of getting to test out his handiwork.

"We are in position," the booming voice squelched from the police scanner. The surveillance feed showed that police had arrived, exited their vehicles with weapons drawn, and were ready to enter the building.

The feed showed the police kick in the door. Michael and Shelbi watched as the officers moved from room to room in the cabin.

"C'mon," Michaels anxiety-filled voice implored as he watched the enemy move around his house. "Turn on a light."

Shelbi remained mute. She watched the men in body armor quickly secure her and Michael's property.

The scanner crackled.

"Clear."

"Anything electrical, anything at all." Michael held his breath while watching the police, who had already begun rifling through his living room desk.

"It'll be the computer they check first," Shelbi whispered. The dilapidated and outdated monstrosity hardly counted as a computer anymore, but she was right. Within seconds of her prediction, a trooper had booted up the machine.

"Yes!" Michael overdramatically extended his arm, as though a wizard casting a spell, before pushing a button on his remote.

A quick spark of ozone wafted up in the cabin, from behind the computer, in the outlet. The trap was simple and made it look like an electrical fire had accidentally occurred in this four-room, bean bag–filled hovel, which was overstuffed with newspapers, magazines, and old junk mail. The overheating wires soon ignited the crawl space, which was filled with "hillbilly insulation": egg cartons, old Styrofoam cushion remnants, and crumpled-up newspaper. The propane tank providing heat to the cabin would explode within minutes. Shelbi would start screaming for help through the intercom just before the propane tank explosion, ensuring that any heroic fool in the rescue party would stay long enough to be evaporated by the blast. Sadly, Michael's older sister Jane, the heroic fool of the family, was not among the rescuers.

"I knew she never cared," Michael muttered, teeth gritted. "Fucking coward. Sending minions to look for her family because she's too busy."

The police scanner crackled. "We have a fire!"

Cautiously, Shelbi asked, "Why no Jane?"

"Because she is a coward." He was disgusted that his older sister didn't care enough to even show up herself. "Bet you killed dad in person."

"What?" Shelbi asked, frightened that Michael was addressing her.

"Not you," he snapped. "Jane. She sent these people. She's looking for us." Leaning back in the chair, arms folded, he said, "Fucking bitch."

"Oh," Shelbi thought, "so we aren't going to try to save Jane?" She felt deep relief that she wasn't the one in Michael's crosshairs.

Michael didn't respond.

"Should we check on Kara?" Shelbi asked. She thought changing the subject might bring down Michael's hackles.

"In a minute, let's watch these people die first." Michael knew Shelbi enjoyed watching people die as much as he did. All couples need shared interests and hobbies.

"OK." Her bubbly and enthusiastic response delighted Michael. "But," she continued, "what do you want to tell Kara? We've had alarms going off, she's locked in your room, she must be feeling trapped and scared."

"She's tougher than she is smart," Michael replied, although neither he nor Shelbi were averting their eyes from the keystone

71

cops who were about to meet their maker. "Just tell her the truth: there was an electrical short, caused the cabin to burn."

The pupils in Michael's eyes expanded as he saw the first microsecond of the propane explosion before the video turned to static. Then, turning, he saw Shelbi—tears of joy were running down her cheeks.

"I love you, Shelbi." His voice was tender and his face reflected the true and real emotion he felt for her.

"I love you more." Her response was equally loving, tender, and genuine.

⟞⟝

Kara was ready. That alarm meant somebody was already looking for her. She could feel it in her bones. "Let's see how Michael and blondie like a little taste of their own medicine." Kara stood by the doorway, syringe in her left hand. "Knock your ass out with your own bullshit zombie drug." Vengeance and derision swirled in her angry voice as she pictured Michael. "And you." Thinking of Shelbi's smiling face. "I'm going to beat you into oblivion." She was going to knock her brother out. Using the faux zombie drug on Michael would be good karma for that little piece of shit. Then the cops could haul him away to Bridgewater, the hospital for the criminally insane.

But the thought of physically destroying Shelbi, that was delicious. That bitch was manipulating and drugging her already-unstable brother. "She won't look like me once I'm done with her." Kara's anger and hate gave her strength. She'd been kidnapped, drugged, lied to, and manipulated. "Once Michael is out she's toast." Going over the inevitable confrontation in her mind over and over. The thought of smashing Shelbi's face made Kara smirk. Kara glanced down at the metal thermos sitting on Michael's desk. "I am going to enjoy this," she thought as she grasped the heavy cylinder with her right hand. "I can't wait to smash blondie's face in."

Kara waited for the door to open. "Any second now," she thought as the alarm echoed in the bunker. "Any second now." She was sure either the cops or her brother would be bursting through that door. She was hoping it wasn't the cops. She wanted payback for what they had done to her.

Time moved like thick syrup on an icy December morning for the woman ready to fight. "C'mon." A syringe in her left hand, behind her back; her right fist clenched hard around the metal thermos. The arm attached to the thermos was taut and ready to hurtle said fist like a rocket-propelled grenade right at Shelbi's face. "C'mon."

Then, the sound—it was the lock! Someone was opening the door. Kara was as tense as a cobra ready to strike its prey. She watched the handle slowly turn.

⇒⟨+ ⟨+⟩

Shelbi smiled as she entered exclaiming, "Everything's OK! We had a fire but it's out."

THWACK!

Shelbi's left bottom front teeth flew across the room with blood following them like the tail of a comet.

Kara felt her middle finger knuckle break as it was crushed between Shelbi's jaw and the thermos-turned-club. The pain in her hand forcing her to drop the weapon.

The sound of skull meeting steel echoed off the metal walls as an unconscious Shelbi's head bounced off the unforgiving floor.

"What the fuck are you doing!" Michael screamed.

The momentum of the right cross Kara threw had turned her back toward the open doorway. Michael had grabbed her from behind as he watched Shelbi fall to the floor. He'd wrapped his arms around Kara and pinned her arms to her side. "Are you crazy?"

Kara's left hand, still grasping a syringe, stuck the needle as deeply and as violently as it could into her brother's thigh. "Fuck you!" she screamed. Her voice was shrill with fury as her thumb pressed down on the plunger. "There—sleep this shit off for a while!"

Michael released her from his iron grip. The fire his flesh felt as the fungal infection coursed its way toward his brain was pale in comparison to the betrayal he felt as he looked at his sister's sneering face.

"You sick son of a bitch!" Kara said. She slapped his face as he fell to his knees. "When you wake up it'll be in a mental ward where you and your fucking bimbo belong!"

"Why?" Michael asked. He couldn't believe his sister had injected him. Numbness began crawling over his body as death began.

"Ask yourself that in prison!" Kara knew she needed to stop yelling and start looking for the keys. She began rifling through the drawers of Michael's ornate desk.

Falling forward. Barely catching himself in time. Michael, now on all fours, stared down at the steel floor. Drool leaking out of his mouth. He felt his breathing becoming shallower with each inhalation. He listed to his right before slumping lifeless into a fetal position.

"God damn it, Michael! Where is the key to this place?" Kara turned drawers upside down and their keyless contents scattered as they bounced and pinged off the steel floor.

Kara looked over and saw her brother lying motionless on the floor. "Sweet dreams, dickhead." Looking at the motionless Shelbi, the pool of blood growing underneath her head, Kara kicked her in the stomach. "Never hit a man when he's down. Kick him—it's easier." Her sister's advice sounded brilliant in her head as her foot made a dull thud against Shelbi's gut.

Kara searched both her brother and Shelbi for the key.

"The TV room." The thought punched her in the face. "Of course, it's in there." Kara tore out of the room and hurried down the hall and into the room lit only by TV monitors. She fumbled along the wall for a light switch, and finding none, she went for the desk in the back. The flickering of Michael's fake Armageddon illuminated the shape of a desktop lamp—Kara turned it on and began tearing apart the workspace. The din of terror coming from the televisions gave Kara a chuckle. "You really had me going for a minute there," she thought. "I almost believed your bullshit zombie story."

BEEEEEEEEEEEEEEEEEEEEEEEEEEEEEEEEEEEEEEEEEEEEE EEE.

The wall of monitors all united in one sound and one image. The words "EMERGENCY ALERT SYSTEM" flashed on every monitor.

"Wow, you're good. This looks real," Kara thought as she glanced at the monitors. "No time." A voice in her head urged her to keep looking.

She grabbed a small drawer and whipped it open. Jangling sounds. "KEYS!" Kara thought.

Two key chains, each with a dozen or so shiny keys attached. Two key cards resembling hotel room passkeys were underneath the traditional metal keys.

"Those." Kara grabbed the plastic cards, instinctively knowing those were the ones. "But just in case." She grabbed the key chains.

Then the unthinkable.

The sound froze her in place. Her breathing stopped, like a gazelle does when anticipating a cheetah attack.

The hairs on the back of her neck stood on end. Gooseflesh overwhelmed her skin.

"Attention!" the voice barked from all the screens at once.

Kara looked up with dread knotting her stomach, knowing what she was about to see.

"My name is Lieutenant Commander Jane Kerr. And I am here to save your lives."

Shock swept Kara. "Jane!!!" Her heart dropped.

ACT 2
TRIBULATION

Her image was clear and crisp on the TV screen in front of Kara.

"My name is Lieutenant Commander Kerr and I am here to save your lives."

Kara, mouth slightly agape, stared at the image of Jane.

"You will be shortly redirected to your local military commander for specific instructions on your area's emergency evacuation plan."

Kara tried denial. "It's a trick. It's CGI. This—it's fake."

"The United States government has fallen."

Denial wasn't working. The voice, the inflection—Kara knew her sister.

"The contrails you see in the sky are from ICBMs. Before Washington fell they launched nukes at the ice caps in Greenland as well as both poles. They believed the resulting tsunamis will wash the dead out to sea."

"Nukes! They launched fucking nukes!"

"The CDC confirmed before they fell that radiation kills the plague. All nuclear plants have been put into meltdown. The radiation from the plants combined with the fallout from the strikes on the ice caps should stop the pandemic spread."

"Meltdown!" Panic began strangling Kara's mind as she watched. "Meltdown?!"

"The first waves will hit the coasts within six hours."

Kara went numb.

"Before I turn this broadcast over to your local commanders, I want you to know we will survive this. The people who have been assigned to oversee your districts are all my troops. We all survived Tokyo. We know how to beat these things. Listen to their instructions," Jane said. Her eyes were ablaze with pride and rage. "And you will live." She saluted the camera. "Your local field commanders will now commence broadcast."

A brief second of snowy static flashed across the screen. A wave of relief began to wash over Kara. "This must be where the tape will loop, proving this isn't real," she thought.

The flash vanished and the image of Jane reappeared. "Lucky you. I am your local field commander," Jane said. The graphic on the screen was a map showing Massachusetts from the New York border to Worcester. "Having a strategic airbases has its advantages when the shit hits the fan."

"This is real." Kara thought. "Only Jane talks like that."

"The tsunami will hit in a matter of hours. Most of the coastal cities are lost. Completely overrun with the infected."

"Hours?"

"We have to prepare for the very real possibility that those waves are going to wash some of those things up on the new shoreline: Westfield."

"No. No! NO! This can't be real!" Kara felt sick.

"Get away from the rivers as fast as you can. Maps of escape routes are on the screen and have just been sent to all of your phones. If, for whatever reason, you cannot get to an escape route, get to the highest point possible in a secure structure and stay quiet. Once we win we will begin sending search and rescue teams for you."

Kara started to hyperventilate. "It's not fake. It's her."

"When we fought these things in Japan we found they have two weaknesses." Jane Kerr's voice intensified as she spoke of her enemies' fatal flaws. "They are attracted to loud noises. And they are afraid of fire. I have troops setting houses ablaze along escape routes. This will help hold them back as you bug out. As for noise, that's where we come in." She motioned to the troops behind her. "My team and I were in Japan when this shit first went down. We know how to fight them. We know how to survive against them. We are going to be bait. We will keep their attention as you make your way to the mountains."

"My sister is going to be bait!"

"My team and I will engage them retreating along Route 20 next to the river. Here, where it meets Route 23, we will make our stand. The sound of our weapons echoing off the mountains and the river valley will draw them for miles." Jane paused, took a deep breath, and continued. "Remember people, we are Americans. We do not lose." A loud "hua-ahh!" erupted from her troops, who were standing behind her. "Evacuation centers have been established and are marked on the maps. Once there you will receive further instructions."

"Oh my God!" The truth kicked Kara hard in the gut. "Michael!"

Kara ran from the room. Around the corner, into the hallway, she grasped the handle to Michael's lair and threw it open.

"Michael!" Her voice rocked by panic as she saw her brother lying motionless on his side. "Michael!" she repeated as she rushed to him. Kneeling beside him, she cradled his head with one hand and checked his jugular for a pulse with the other.

No pulse and his flesh felt cold.

"The antidote." Kara scanned the room for where the cylinder had fallen after her attack on Shelbi. "It's not too late!" Gently, but quickly, she laid her brother flat on the floor and then scrambled toward the thermos, which was lying under a table. She grabbed the thermos and tried to unscrew it. Her swollen knuckle shot electricity up her arm.

Kara froze. Her spine was ice.

She turned around and saw Michael sit up. His torso rose unnaturally as if pulled up by puppet strings. His head and shoulders turned slowly toward her.

Their eyes locked, and Kara's dilated—the first fight-or-flight symptom fear produces in the human nervous system.

Michael's unblinking eyes stared straight ahead, frozen perfectly forward. His pupils and irises were covered in a milky film, courtesy of the full fungal infestation.

Kara's scream was primal and uncontrollable. The adrenaline flushing through her system prepared her muscles for escape.

Michael's scream was paralyzing—the audio she had heard on the news broadcasts had done no justice to the piercing volume and horrific timbre it produced. Kara's eardrums felt like hot needles were being jammed into them. The scream vibrated her bones violently

With all her might, and without conscious thought, she hurled the thermos at her brother's snarling, shrieking face.

The sound of metal cracking Michael's teeth crawled up Kara's back like a snake. The force broke most of his teeth—some flew intact out of his head, while others became nothing more than jagged, razor-sharp enamel shards.

Kara bolted for the doorway and jumped to avoid the unconscious Shelbi. She raced out the door.

Michael's eyes were frozen forward and his fungus-infested body was manipulating his head to follow his prey's flight. His scream intensified with each step Kara took, and so did his smell. His body began decomposing and expelling all waste matter and digestive juices. The bile-urine-feces cocktail oozed down his legs.

As he rose, his blood, which would have normally pooled in his back as he lied dead on the floor, now drained into his feet. Each stuttering step the barefoot corpse took created lesions. The tears in his flesh widened, spewing blackened blood onto the floor that left a slick trail in the monster's wake.

Kara yanked on the handle for the door. It didn't budge.

"No lock?!" Kara frantically looked, but there was no keyhole, no card swipe, nothing. The carcass of her sibling was only a few feet from her now. The shrill scream it made caused her to shudder.

Kara looked over her left shoulder at the open door she had fled through. In the reflection of the steel walls she could see that Michael was right behind her.

"Move!" Fight or flight kicked Kara into gear. The hand of the carcass missed her by inches as it swiped for its prey.

Kara fled toward the temple. The smell coming off Michael's cadaver was so strong that she could taste it in the back of her throat.

The corpse's head tracked his prey as it fled down the hallway—its gait alternated between striding and shuffling as it gave chase. The fungus was seemingly unsure on whether this carrion suit would be of the slow or fast variety.

Kara slammed the heavy temple door behind her, creating a cascading sound of hissing and rattling that washed down the sides of the cave. "Again! No lock! Fuck!" Kara had no way to secure the door other than to lean her back into it.

The handle turned and Kara felt the weight of her brother's dead body push on the other side. Over 6 feet tall, barrel-chested, and weighing around 220 pounds, her brother's corpse could not be held back long. The blood still leaking from his feet provided slippery footing for the monster as he pushed. Its feet gripped the floor better with each second as the bones from its toes began scratching at and then gripping the floor

Kara's thoughts formed fast. "Leap." It seemed like a good idea leap to her left. Michael, pushing hard on the other side, would fall down, and she could jump over him to get back to his room—she knew that the door in that room had a lock. She looked to her left, then to her right. Corpses of Michael's followers, their skulls shattered, lay covered in white powder. The bodies contorted on the cavern floor, the lye not seeming to bother the angry vipers that were slithering across them. Her brother's screaming, even through the heavy oak door, seemed to bring the rattlesnakes out of their hibernation.

"Fuck! Jumping on rattlesnakes is never a good plan." Kara looked toward the altar. "Run toward it and look for a weapon—these things are slow and clumsy. Move it."

"What if he's a fast one?" She hesitated at the thought.

"Then move faster!" She snapped back at herself while darting toward the stalagmite with her brother's smiling face carved on it.

BAM!

The heavy oak door flew open, barely missing the fleeing woman as it did. The thunderous sound of it smashing against rock, combined with the unholy scream booming from the dead body, sent the snakes into a rage. The rattling of their tails combining with the monster's howl created a deafening cacophony that echoed throughout the cave.

Kara didn't feel her feet touch the stone floor as she ran. Reaching the altar, she saw a lone copy of the book of Michael sitting on the shelves that were carved into the back of the stalagmite. Kara turned around to see Michael's corpse shuffling toward her and took in what had happened to him: His skin was gray and devoid of all blood. His flesh looked as though it was trying to slide off his face. His mouth was half-filled with broken teeth that looked more animal than human. His unblinking eyes were locked on Kara's.

His steel-gray eyes that were so striking in life now blended with his pallid flesh. Never blinking. The pupils were shrunken to the size of a pinprick. Kara could feel the evil coming off this thing as easily as she could smell its decaying tissue.

"Can't get around him." Snakes to the right and left of her, Kara knew there was only one way out. "Gotta go through him."

Reaching down, she grabbed the thick religious tome, opened it to the halfway mark, and placed her left forearm in the open book. Her right hand tightly grasped pages with her fingers, the front leather cover lying across her swelling knuckle. The thumb and palm of her hand squeezed the leather cover and the book's contents hard against her forearm, forming a bracer. She held her newly minted leather-and-paper armor up to shield her face as she ran toward Michael's dead body.

Michael slowly and steadily shambled toward the woman racing toward him. The scream the monster made was so loud it physically hurt Kara as she ran at it.

Kara let out her own war scream as she smashed her book-covered forearm directly into the creature's open mouth. The force of her leaping at the corpse caused Michael to tumble backward. His jaw snapped with the intensity of a bear trap on the book's spine; his jaw and teeth—no longer limited by pain—kept crushing together. Kara's arm was on the brink of snapping in two under the strain. As they hit the cavern floor, Kara was somersaulted over Michael's head and she released her grip on the book,

Kara landed hard on her tailbone. Her head swiveled and she expected to see her brother ready to pounce on her. Instead, she saw his carcass impaled, slowly sliding down a stalagmite. His torso was ripping from his hips and legs the farther it slid down the sharp stone pillar. His hands and legs were thrashing for freedom, further causing his already-decaying flesh to rip and tear. To Kara he looked like an insect going through its death throes while trapped in a spider's web.

She stopped breathing as she felt the first rattlesnake slither across her broken knuckle.

The second snake quickly wriggled across her outstretched legs. Kara watched as a third seemed to fly over her, barely touching her on its way to striking Michael's screaming corpse. Twisting and turning to free itself from its impalement, the corpse was being repeatedly struck as if by bullwhips by the five-foot-long rattlesnakes. Their fangs instinctively retracted once they tasted Michael's dead flesh, only to ready themselves for another attack as the cadaver's screaming caused the snakes' nervous system to overload, similar to a shark in a feeding frenzy.

The corpse, unfazed by the growing throng of rattlesnakes puncturing its flesh, twisted with the sickening sound of skin ripping and bones breaking. The two halves of Michael's body fell to the floor. His legs lay motionless. His torso slowly reached out its hands. Grabbing at the slimy cave floor, the torso began to crawl toward Kara, whose outstretched legs were soon covered with a river of vipers that were racing toward her brother.

Kara began standing as slowly as she could. Michael's corpse was five feet away and closing in. The snakes' strikes slammed into his torso. His progress was hindered as the force from the enraged vipers' attack slid the shrieking corpse along the algae-covered cavern floor.

Kara watched the snakes as she rose. The river of reptilians slid over and under her legs. Michael was inching closer, but Kara was rising steadily—the snakes couldn't care less about her and she knew it. Michael was only two feet away now. She pulled herself with her right hand up toward the walkway. Swinging her feet up, she rolled herself onto the walkway and got to her feet. She looked down at her brother's torso as it grasped and clawed its way toward her.

Its eyes looked directly into Kara's. She saw the unblinking, unfeeling eyes. There was no Michael in there. Her baby brother was gone.

She turned toward the exit. "Michael's dead." The thought punched her. "And you killed him." Flinging open the door she moved quickly toward the exit, she thought, "I have the cure in my blood. I have to get to my sister."

Kara again tried the latch to no avail. "God damn it!" Reaching in her shirt pocket, she felt the key cards. The key rings were long gone—they'd been thrown from her pocket by the summersault she took while fighting Michael. "C'mon, you have to work!" she thought while swiping one card, then another through the doorjamb, desperately hoping for something to happen. "Fuck!"

Frustration racking her thoughts, Kara took the two cards, placed them together so the magnetic strips were facing out, and swiped them through the doorjamb.

CLICK.

Kara turned the latch and the heavy steel door swung open. She heard Shelbi staggering into the hallway behind her.

Kara looked at the wounded woman. "IT WAS THE COPS!" she screamed at the dazed and bleeding blonde. "FLASH GRENADES! MICHAEL IS IN THE TEMPLE! HE'S HURT!"

Shelbi stared at Kara, her concussed brain struggling hard to clear the cobwebs choking it.

"HE'S HURT! HE NEEDS YOU!"

Shelbi nodded, her brain unable to fully process information. "Michael needs me," she thought as she slowly staggered toward the temple.

Kara saw that the open doorway led to a ladder. Entering the exit way, she quickly grasped the rungs, her forearm throbbing where Michael had tried to bite her. She flew up the twelve feet and entered a circular steel storeroom filled with various supplies.

"Are you kidding me?!"

There was no door, no way out. Looking up, Kara saw a small air vent. "Fuck!" Her source of fresh air was the ventilation system. Kara turned and slid down the ladder.

Reentering the hallway, she heard Shelbi screaming. "Good!" Kara thought. She then turned and ran down the steel hallway opposite the direction of the temple. She heard Shelbi's screaming going up several octaves behind her as she fled.

The hallway came to a T intersection. To her left, Kara saw doors. Lots of doors. To her right she saw only three. Her instinct told her, "Go right." Left had to be the dormitory.

There were three doors—one on each side of her and one in front of her, at the end of the short hallway, which she darted for.

"Locked!"

She first turned to her left, flinging open the door—it was dark and the air was musty. She hit a light switch by the door and row after row of fluorescent lights came to life, illuminating the huge mushroom farm.

Kara spun around and headed for the door opposite this one. Flinging the door open, the sight that greeted her in Michael's library stopped her dead in her tracks: a huge aquarium that was built into the far wall. Engraved on a four-foot brass plaque hanging above the aquarium were the words "Martyr's Tank" in slightly smaller font underneath the title. "For those who sacrificed all. So that the world be Free of Evil" was scrawled. She remembered Michael's words: "Occasionally the antidote doesn't take." The decapitated heads floating inside the formaldehyde-filled tank were tethered in place. Floating helplessly, they snarled and snapped their jaws at the sight of Kara.

"MOVE!!!" her mind screamed.

Kara rushed back into the hallway, back to the locked door. That's when she saw the keypad next to the steel gateway.

"OK, Michael. What did you use?"

She knew her brother. For all his brilliance he was unbelievably shitty at password security. "Think…you can get this."

Her first try was "G-O-D-Z-I-L-L-A," his favorite monster as a kid.

Red light…no good.

Her second try—"R-O-M-E-R-O"—was his favorite movie director.

Green light...click.

"Fuck yeah!" the thrill shot of adrenaline she got as the door swung open turned to gooseflesh as she noticed Shelbi's screams were gone and only the horrible shrieks of Michael's corpse filled the hallways behind her.

Flinging open the door, she saw a ladder, which led up to a hatchway that looked like it belonged on a submarine.

Electric shards of pain shot through Kara's left arm as she began climbing. Even though Michael's teeth couldn't get through his unholy tome the sheer pressure his jaws had exerted on her arm had left a hideous bone bruise, the pain of which, could not be ignored.

"C'mon. Don't break. Don't break." Kara felt her willpower was the only thing keeping her arm from snapping in two as she ascended.

Kara reached the top of the ladder and hooked her left elbow on the top rung. Her left forearm burned as if the bones within had been ignited. With her right hand she began turning the round wheel of the latch.

It turned with ease.

CLICK.

She pushed up, and the spring-loaded door flew open.

Fresh air cascaded into the shaft. Kara scrambled up the last few rungs and emerged into a cave entrance. Kara ran out the opening in the mountainside. The icy temperature slapped her skin hard as she emerged from her subterranean prison.

She scanned her surroundings. No house, no car, just woods.

"Where am I?" To her right she the saw smoke rising over the tree line from Michael's booby-trapped house.

"Not that way," her gut instructed. Kara began running straight ahead. The memory of her nightmare rose up on her as she fled.

The trees swayed in the cold December wind and their barren branches danced above Kara as she ran for her life.

"Focus!" she screamed while attempting to suppress the memories of her nightmare.

She had the antidote in her blood. She was the key to saving the world. She knew that.

Two words formed a mantra within Kara as she ran. Two words that shut out the terror. The image of her sister on TV flashed in her mind's eye as she kept repeating: "Find her!"

⚔

The war room underneath Barnes Air National Guard Base was a hurricane and Lieutenant Commander Jane Kerr was its eye. Local police and firefighters combined with military and civilian volunteers were working seamlessly together and formed the last fighting force Kerr would ever command. And Kerr couldn't be happier with their progress, although you couldn't tell that by the way she was barking out orders.

"Where are we on those fires?" Kerr asks.

"Crews have fire line along the northern and southern riverbanks set to go at your order ma'am," the fire chief answered.

"Update on evacuations."

"Ma'am, we have a problem," a very young soldier answered.

"What?" Kerr snapped.

"People are gathering in the center of town by the big church," the soldier explained. "They are refusing to evacuate. And the crowd is growing, ma'am."

Kerr picked up her helmet—Sharpied across the front of it was her nickname, "GRANDMA," which referred to her shiny platinum hair. While placing it on her head, she said, "Let's go, soldier."

"Yes ma'am."

≈+ +≈

Kerr surveyed the deserted neighborhoods as her convoy of five Humvees sped toward the center of town. Even with a low infection rate, these usually idyllic suburban neighborhoods showed the tell-tale scars of battle. Burned-out vehicles lay abandoned on lawns and bullet-scarred vinyl siding surrounded broken and blood-stained windows, giving Kerr the impression she was in Mogadishu instead of Massachusetts.

"Update on coastline," Kerr's voice growled over the radio. "Over."

"Tsunami, five hundred klicks offshore, should hit coast within the half hour," Genevieve's familiar voice answered back. "Computer projects debris field will hit us thirty to forty-five minutes after that."

"Fuck, that's ahead of schedule," Kerr thought.

"Refugee numbers for the camp?" Kerr asked.

Genevieve looked down at her laptop. "Either the infection rate here was much higher than forecast, or a lot of people are trying to go it alone," she answered.

"If things go sideways I need you to keep those people safe."

Genevieve glanced around the interior of the MRAP (Mine Resistant Armored Protected) vehicle she was inside of. Kerr's reasoning behind ordering her to run the drone strikes from a mobile unit inside the refugee camp was twofold: one, to decentralize command structure—if the airbase went sideways, the drone strikes would be unaffected; and two, if Kerr's position went sideways, then she had someone she had confidence in to keep the civilians alive.

"Roger that, ma'am," Genevieve replied.

The smell of gasoline-drenched businesses filled Kerr's airways as they approached the twin bridges. "Once we are over the river light up on the north side of town," Kerr said.

"Roger that," Genevieve replied. "Drones locked and loaded, ma'am."

"Update on the F-15s."

"Alpha squadron in position, ma'am."

As the last of Kerr's convoy crossed into the battle scarred south side of town, magnesium flares dropped from the drones, igniting the gasoline-soaked structures. Thick black smoke choked out the sunlight behind the convoy as it moved toward its destination.

As the convoy rounded the corner onto Elm Street, Kerr finally saw the gathering crowd.

"Here's the deal, ladies," Kerr snarled over the intercom. "If we can't get these people to leave voluntarily…and we probably can't. We are going to have to set up a defensive perimeter around them."

Kerr didn't need to see the puzzled looks on the faces of her men—she knew what they were thinking. It was a waste of time and resources to try to save people who don't want it.

"We save everybody, people." Her words were harsh, almost scolding. "This is a numbers game. The more people alive and fighting, the better chance we all have of living. Once these things start getting close the sound and smell of them will make most of these people shit their pants and run for the hills anyway." Scanning the crowd as well as the downtown landscape, she continued. "It's our job to give these people a fighting chance to escape." Kerr looked at a street map of Westfield in her HUD and began positioning her troops. "We have fires started on East Main Street from Mainline Drive to Little River Road. I need East Silver Street, Noble Ave, and Meadow Street up to Mechanic Street lit up. Keep Court Street clear for these people's retreat."

"Roger." Three of the five Humvees peeled off toward their assignments. Kerr's vehicle slowed as it reached the edge of the crowd.

⚒ ⚒

The crowd turned as if on cue to look at the military vehicle. The faces staring at Kerr were hollow and scared into a stupor. Tear-filled eyes stared at Kerr. This was the same look she saw in the eyes of Somali refugees only a few months before in Africa. It was the look of those resigned to death. To see it on the people of her hometown broke Kerr's heart and tripled her resolve.

The crowd slowly began to part, allowing the Humvee to get closer to the church. People in the crowd began yelling at the slowly moving truck.

"We are fine."

"I love you."

"Thank you."

"God be with you."

Then, the most unexpected sound: applause.

"At least it's not a hostile crowd, ma'am," the young driver said.

"That can change," Kerr replied sternly.

The Humvee came to a halt at the front steps of the church. The priest walking down the steps toward them was in his sixties. He was bald on top and his remaining hair was short and white. His eyes twinkled with kindness from underneath his round wire-rimmed glasses.

"We were expecting you," the man said. His voice was hoarse from hours of comforting the scared. "Welcome." His arms were open and ready for an embrace.

Kerr exited the vehicle, removed her helmet, and approached the man. "Sir," she said. Her tone was respectful but firm.

"Please, call me Father, my child," the man said. He clasped his hands together, seeing from her body language that an embrace was not going to happen.

"Father." Kerr didn't miss a beat. "We have to get these people out of here."

While holding up his hands and smiling, the white-collared man warmly replied, "I thought you'd say that." He looked over

93

at the armored vehicle and continued: "Does this have a loud-speaker in it? Something we can use to address the crowd. These people are frightened. I think it's important to let them hear this conversation."

Kerr looked back around at the shell-shocked faces behind her. Fear emanated from the crowd like heat off asphalt on an August afternoon. With the exception of a few simpering infants, the crowd was now silent. The sound of a choir wafted out the open doors of the church.

"Turn on the PA," she barked at the driver, who quickly obeyed. The driver opening his door, flipped a switch on the dash, and then stood at attention and nodded confirmation to his commander.

Kerr pressed on her left wrist where a pulse would be. A clicking sound followed by a quick squelch of feedback blasted from the Humvee—the automatic audio adjustment unit quickly compensated, and Kerr's voice boomed from the vehicle.

"This area is not safe," Kerr said into the microphone on her wrist. "I need you to all evacuate immediately."

"Please, my daughter." The priest had stepped close enough for her microphone to pick up his speaking, just as he had hoped. "These people know what's happening. The question is, do you?"

"The first waves will start hitting the coasts in the next few minutes. Within an hour the rivers will start flowing backward. That's when—"

"The sea shall give up her dead," the priest said, interrupting her. "Yes, we know. It is written in Revelations. It is the sign that final judgment has begun."

"With all due respect, Father," Kerr said. Her tone was polite and didn't give away how much she wanted to slap that smarmy smile off the old man's face. "Unless the next line is the sea shall give up her dead, and then they will eat you, I don't think we are talking about the same event. These things are monsters. They eat people. It is a horrible and brutal way to die, and I've seen a lot of death, sir. This is not anything that came from any God, this is a bio-attack of some kind and we have to get these people to safety."

"With all due respect, my daughter. To say that corpses rising from the dead have any other explanation than an angry God is neither logical nor realistic. Listen to yourself my child. Listen to your heart. You know I'm speaking the truth. Please stay with us in love and fellowship as our judgment approaches."

"I'm sorry, Father, but here's the reality of the situation. First you are going to smell these things probably while they are still several miles away. Then as they move closer the screams become audible. Then they attack."

"We've seen the footage, my child."

"Yes, sir, you have, but I lived it. I fought my way out of Japan. Me and my team are proof we can beat these things. Look, Father, if you are right—if this is the apocalypse—then nothing I can do or say is going to possibly stop it. Whether these people decide to flee to the hills or stay here, the same outcome occurs. If, however, I'm right and you are wrong, you are sentencing these innocent people to a horrendously brutal and needless death. Please, Father, I'm trying to save these people."

"So am I, my child. You're trying to save their flesh. I'm trying to save something more important: their souls."

"I can't make you leave." She was done with the passive-aggressive old man. Kerr now appealed to the crowd directly. "But I am begging you, please go. What is coming is worse than you can imagine."

The crowd stood silent.

"My men are rigging incendiary devices in this location, except Court Street—that's your best escape route."

The crowd was mostly silent. However, a slight murmur began to emerge as Kerr continued.

"We don't have to die. We can beat these things, people. We can. I've done it once I can do it again. If I'm wrong the world ends. If I'm right, when we beat these things, we will have saved the world."

The scared murmur was steady but soft underneath her speech.

"If you wish to go!" The priest shouted loud enough to be heard through the mic on Kerr's wrist. "You should go with her!" Kerr, stunned by the priest's declaration, turned to see the old man smiling.

"May I?" he asked while motioning toward the mic. Kerr nodded and held her wrist out to him.

"My children." Tears glistened the old man's eyes. His tone was gentle and sweet. "If you are unsure. If you have doubts. By all means you can go with...no, no, I'm sorry. You should go with her."

Scattered gasps came from the throng.

"If there is one thing I believe in...that I know to be true is, God forgives. He forgave Peter three times as he denied his Son. I can't imagine he wouldn't forgive you for being scared," he said and smiled reassuringly. "Or for trying to stay alive. I will be here, tending to my flock. You all are welcome to stay, and any who wish to leave, please do so knowing that God loves you," he said and glanced at Kerr. "He gave us free will for a reason. I'm sure he will forgive whoever makes the wrong choice." The priest moved his hands in the sign of the cross and nodded at Kerr.

"If you want the best chance of living you need to leave now," Kerr said and pressed her left wrist.

The crowd began talking in hushed and urgent tones. There was movement as some people immediately began moving out of the crowd and toward the escape route. Others choosing to stay simply embraced their loved ones. The movement of people leaving looked like streams of water running from a delta from Kerr's perspective on top of the church stairs.

"I'll fight," a lone voice from the crowd said. Kerr scanned quickly and saw Jaden, the scrawny kid in a puffy blue down jacket. Kerr motioned the teen to approach.

"I'll fight," he repeated as he approached.

"Can you shoot, kid?" Kerr asked.

"Yeah, been hunting with my uncle my whole life."

"Good, what I need is for you to do is stay alive, go straight up Court Street, keep heading up the hills, if you can get any more of these people to follow you all the better."

"But I want to fight, I want to help."

"Get to the hills. We have troops up there digging in for a fight. You'll get your chance, kid."

"Ma'am," the driver interjected. "Look."

Kerr looked to see some people from inside the church leaving. Certainly not all, but at least some.

Kerr saw the priest approaching her. "Thank you, Father." Kerr wanted every last person out of there, and was not going to scale back the defenses her troops were preparing near the church. But she also knew when to accept victory, even partial ones.

"It's called free will, my child," the pontiff retorted. "I'm sure it's something you wouldn't understand being in the military. I know they drum that out of you people."

"How's your God feel about passive-aggressive bullshit, padre?" a pissed-off Kerr shot back.

"Though I walk through the shadow of the valley of death I shall fear no evil, knowing the Lord is with me," the priests said in a triumphant tone.

"I don't fear evil, Father," Kerr replied. "I'm US military. I fight evil. And I defeat it. "

The priest snapped a fierce look at Kerr then turned to see the small portion of the gathered flock begin to peel off. "I will pray for you, my daughter."

Kerr stared at the old man. "Thanks," she replied flatly.

She turned to Jaden and said, "Go, kid. I'll see you soon."

"I can shoot. I can help."

"I know, kid. Now get going. That's an order!"

"Yes sir…umm I mean ma'am."

Kerr put her helmet on, entered the vehicle, and slammed the door. "Lieutenant commander, we have a problem," a voice said over the radio.

"What is it?" Kerr replied.

"The river, ma'am," the scared soldier respond. "It's starting to flow backward."

—×··×—

Pain tore into Kara's side, it hit her like a linebacker as she ran for her life. Her muscles jerked, causing her to double over.

"Go!"

Her legs—fueled by fear—pushed her, even as she fell forward, crashing to the snow-covered ground.

Gasping hard for air as she fell, she was afraid that her nightmare was prophetic. She looked behind her for pursuers. No one in sight. She listened…nothing. New England winters, as brutal as they can be, are never able to wring the songs of birds or the chatter of squirrels out of the woods.

These woods had no sound.

"It's dead," Kara thought, her heart pounding in her ears. "MOVE!"

Kara scrambled back to her feet, obeying her brain's primitive command.

The stitch in her side brutalized her. Every movement her body made felt attached to her side now, and every movement hurt.

"Corner of Route 20 and 23." Kara knew exactly where her sister would be.

Route 20 was a winding, narrow road that cut along the side of the Berkshires—one side was buffeted by sheer one-hundred-foot granite walls; on the other side, a cliff plunged a hundred feet down to jagged granite boulders that protruded from the Westfield River.

"Best spot for it. A last stand," Kara thought as she visualized the sharp incline of where Route 23 joined 20 in a T. "It's perfect." She remembered driving that road. How the incline felt like a roller coaster slowly approaching its first plunge. The granite walls on Route 23 loomed over you, giving you the sense of what trash must feel like before being compacted. "Perfect kill box." She knew her sister would pick the best place to win this fight.

"We can stop this!" The antidote flowed through her—she knew she was the last hope of stopping this thing. "Get to her! We can stop this!" She repeated the mantra again and again. It gave her brain something to focus on other than the excruciating pain from her side and now her arm. Up until this moment, she hadn't realized how bad the injuries to her arm were. "What the fuck did I do?" she thought as she looked at her broken left forearm. "Probably climbing the ladder out of the bunker," she replied to herself. "You're in shock, it's why you can't feel it."

Kara placed her right hand on the break, which was midway up her left forearm. She gritted her teeth and snapped the bone back together. The shooting electricity of pain that travelled from her arm to her brain went sailing out Kara's mouth with an earsplitting scream of pain as she fell.

Kara looked to the side of the snow-covered dirt road. "Branches!"

Kara scrambled up, reaching the side of the road she unfastened her belt. Having no shortage of broken branches to choose from she quickly fastened a crude but effective splint for her left arm.

The hair on the back of her neck straightened as she heard a scream echo off the mountain behind her. The direction the scream was coming from was unclear. Kara was aware of only two things now: One, the sound was from one of those things. And two, it was getting closer.

⇥ ⇤

The smell was unmistakable. The dead were approaching, and judging by the stench, they weren't far.

"Repeat that, soldier!" Kerr snapped into her intercom.

"The river is starting to flow backward, ma'am," the young soldier's voice crackled back at her through intermittent static. "Over."

"Talk to me, Genevieve."

"Satellite data shows wave has already hit East Coast. Rapidly approaching inland position."

"What the fuck, Genevieve!"

"Satellite data has been spotty, systems are failing worldwide, ma'am. Original data was incorrect."

"Everyone, fall back to corner Route 20 and Elm." Jane's command rang out over the radio. "Go!" she barked at her driver.

The Humvee roared to life, tires ripping up chunks of the flimsy asphalt street as it tore into reverse to escape the crowd.

The driver turned the wheel hard as they emerged from the throng, then slammed the beast into drive and sped the Humvee down the street, knocking over a traffic light as though it were made of paper instead of steel.

"We have enemy contact!" The voice on the radio was shrill with battle. "Twin bridges, enemy in water, and there's a lot of them."

"Go! Go! Go!" Jane said while pointing toward the bridges just up the road from the rendezvous point.

Jane—a veteran of wars and covert ops and the first to fight and win against the undead—couldn't believe her eyes as they turned the corner.

The inferno, on the far side of the river, backlit the battle with a fifty-foot wall of flame. A thick black ceiling of smoke choked

100

out the sky above. Her men were laying down constant suppressive fire at the river bank. Body after gray body flung itself up toward the attack, only to be torn apart under the torrent of hot lead. The bodies kept coming and coming—the rate was faster than back in Japan. So many corpses were crawling up the riverbank that the gunfire ripping them to pieces was barely slowing their ascent. Cadavers crawled over the bank and one another. The ferocity of the gunfire increased as Jane and her crew unleashed more fire-power at the monsters.

"Bug out! Bug out!" Genevieve's voice screamed over the radio. "SEWERS! They are coming up through the sewers! You're being outflanked!"

"Let's go! Let's go! Let's go!" Jane's voice cracked like a whip. Her troops jumped into their vehicles and the convoy screamed back toward Route 20.

Rounding the corner, Jane saw the dead bubbling up from the sewer at the corner of Elm Street and Route 20. Beyond that, less than two hundred yards up the road, the crowd seeking refuge at the church was already being torn to shreds. The throng writhed in agony as some fought, some fled, and some simply did nothing but scream as the dead devoured them.

"Gun it," Kerr ordered.

The driver pressed the accelerator, shooting their Humvee straight at the corpses, smashing the dead that were charging at them. Turning hard to the right, the vehicle crushed the charging cadavers as it turned off Elm and onto 20. The Humvee's wheels liquefied those misfortunate enemies who fell beneath them.

"Form up!" Kerr said. Her voice was steady and calm. Three Humvees sped in front of Jane's vehicle forming a V shape. Another Humvee pulled alongside Jane's. Jane popped open the hatch to the gun turret. She looked to her left—Sergeant Cornelius, the best shot she knew, was at the ready already positioned in the gun turret of the Humvee alongside hers'.

"Locked and loaded, ma'am," his voice sounded in her ear. Jane readied herself and the fifty-caliber machine gun in front of her. "Time to send these fuckers back to hell!"

⊶ ⊷

Kara didn't move a muscle, fearing the slightest twitch might snap a branch or rustle a dead leaf alerting the fiend of her location. The options were bad. Her broken arm meant she couldn't climb. The fresh snow cover meant as soon as she started running there would be no way of hiding her location. Freshly fallen snow has a certain crunchiness to it, and crunchy sounds are always loud.

The screaming sound hissed as it echoed through the woods. Kara couldn't fathom where in the woods it was coming from, or how close it may be.

POP! POP! POP! POP!

Kara had spent time with her sister at the range. She knew the sound of automatic gunfire. She also knew by the faintness of the sound that it was quite far away.

The screaming sound grew distant. The sound of gunfire drew the unseen zombie—the corpse staggered toward the distant noise.

Kara realized as she stood that something remarkable had occurred while she had lain frozen on the ground.

She had gained her second wind.

Kara started running faster than she ever had in her life.

"Get to her! We can stop this!" A fresh shot of adrenaline dulled the pain of her injuries.

POP! POP! POP!

The gunfire echoed through the empty forest as Kara made her way toward the river. Her sister would be on the other side. "Get to her!" Kara's brain wasn't allowing the reality of her situation to be a distraction. Thoughts about her brother and what he had truly done were quickly stamped down in her brain. "We can stop this!" Her survival dictated a singular purpose. "Get to her!" Everything else was too much to deal with.

Another scream echoed through the woods—it seemed close, but Kara didn't care. The sound of gunfire to the south would draw it away from her. "Get to her." She was at the end of the snowy dirt road that led to Michael's property. The pothole-riddled street ran parallel to the river. To her left was the sound of gunfire and seven miles away, a bridge crossing the waterway. To her right: three or so miles of snowy roadway until the next crossing, a foot-bridge closed for safety concerns. Less than half a mile in front of her, through a small thicket of woods, was the river.

"Winter. The river is low." Kara knew that at this time of year the river couldn't be more than a few inches above her knees. It was probably mostly frozen over in many spots. "Go! It's your best chance!" Kara plunged into the woods and sank in the snow up to her calves as brambles and twigs clawed at her face as though trying to hold her back. She trudged hard through the snow, planning her next move. "Hopefully not steep!" Most of the Route 20 side of the riverbank was steep. There were a few spots where the roadway followed the landscape and dipped down close to the river. These contours were few and far between—Kara was holding onto the hope that one of these contours would be near where she emerged.

She broke through the thicket to see the steep cliff on the other side of the Westfield River, which was now rising and flowing backward.

The shriek she heard coming from her left was no echo. She turned to see a screaming corpse rising up on her side of the river-bank, its eyes locked on her, snarling as it ran straight at her.

—◄+ +►—

A fifty-caliber machine gun has a rhythm to it when used properly.

Squeeze the trigger, say to yourself, "DIE MOTHERFUCKER DIE" as the bullets let loose.

Then breathe…let off the trigger…one thousand one…one thousand two…Repeat.

The breathing part keeps the blistering heat of firing the weapon manageable and keeps it from melting the weapon's barrel.

"DIE MOTHERFUCKER DIE!" Jane squeezed off her rounds then paused as Sergeant Cornelius to her left opened fire. Alternating back and forth, they unleashed hell on the enemies chasing them. The Humvees in front of them formed a wedge and smashed the few vehicles littering the roadway out of their path.

"DIE MOTHERFUCKER DIE." Fifty-caliber weapons are meant to stop armored vehicles, turning them into flaming hunks of twisted metal resembling Swiss cheese.

It turns people into a pink mist.

As the corpses were cut down by heavy machine-gun fire, they turned not into a fine pink mist but into a cloud of dark-gray vapor.

"How fuckin' many of these things are there, Genevieve?" Jane screamed as she counted in her head, "One thousand one…one thousand two." The NSA computers had calculated the worst-case scenario: 250,000 dead washing up over a 12-hour period.

DIE MOTHERFUCKER DIE.

"Genevieve!"

The Sergeant, her heart in her throat, stared at the feed coming in from the drone. The rising water was boiling with corpses. The approaching water was so thick with the undead that it looked more like a marathon than a tsunami.

"Millions, ma'am."

"What?" Jane thought she'd misheard.

"The water is seething with them, ma'am"

DIE MOTHERFUCKER DIE. The shots rang out. "It looks like I'm shooting at water." Jane yelled. The dead were charging fast. The rising water was within inches of cresting the Westfield River's bank, providing the dead easy access to dry land and their prey. The corpses swarmed out of the water with the ferocity of angry hornets, racing toward the sound of incoming fire. Each of the fifty-caliber rounds exploded hundreds of zombies.

One thousand one...one thousand two...and there they were again, closer to Jane than before—not by much, but still closer. Charging so fast, they seemed to form out of the pallid fog that had been their unholy brethren.

"I suggest airstrikes, ma'am." The screen in front of Sergeant Genevieve showed a bird's-eye perspective on the hellscape. Corpses...uncountable numbers...miles of corpses. They were not just in the water, being carried along like flotsam—they were moving with the water. The rising rivers were so thick with the dead that they seemed devoid of liquid. The fast ones streamed from the riverbank like foam escaping a wave and crashing ashore.

"Not yet."

DIE MOTHERFUCKER DIE. The undead hordes' teeth-splintering scream threatened to drown out the machine-gun fire. And Jane's reply.

"Do you read me, Genevieve?"

"Loud and clear, ma'am," Genevieve replied.

DIE MOTHERFUCKER DIE. The burning CLP gun lube, coming off the weapon, mingled with the smell of tons of decaying flesh in Jane's nostrils as she replied.

"Good...start lighting the fence...I want these mountains ringed with fire."

"On it, ma'am." Genevieve began attacking her keyboard. Her lightning-fast fingers sent drones strafing Westfield with incendiary bullets. The rounds, miniature versions of fuel-air explosives, contained enough chemicals to set ten football fields ablaze. And they were now reigning down on strategic points throughout town in order to funnel the enemy into the kill box.

"Convoy, keep it steady," Jane barked through the intercom. "Thirty-five until I say."

The dead hurtled toward the convoy with Olympian speed on their kamikaze date with the molten fifty-caliber rounds that ended their brief but brutal afterlife.

"Enemy ahead!" Jane's head swiveled as the voice blared the alert through the radio. Route 20 dipped and rose like a rollercoaster in several places as it followed the contours of the granite cliff face it was blasted into. The first of these dips was by the golf course, which was already three-quarters flooded—there, a swarm of snarling dead streamed ashore and headed straight for the convoy.

"Clear 'em out!" Jane's voice rang out clearly over the barrage of heavy machine-gun fire.

Roof hatches on the three lead convoys flew open, and warriors at the ready opened fire. The sound of the hell they unleashed echoed like thunder through the river valley. The convoy still pressed forward and began to drive through the gray vapor left by the obliterated enemies, coating the vehicles and warriors in a thin, slimy mist.

DIE MOTHERFUCKER DIE.

Kara stood her ground as the corpse approached.

The dead man's pallid lips curled into a snarl, bearing its yellowing teeth. All traces of humanity had been washed from its face. This was pure predator—a killing machine that was closing in.

Kara stood ready to fight. Every ounce of adrenaline that had fueled her escape now powered her anger.

The dead man's snarl contorted, curling upward as it bared its teeth. It leaped at her.

Kara formed her right hand into a talon as she struck at its face. Her thumb plunged into the creature's left eye, which felt like rotten fruit as it popped and leaked down her wrist. Her fingers clamped down on the slimy skin of its forehead, forming a viselike grip on its skull. Her arm out straight, elbow locked. The zombie's head tilted backward as its body continued forward.

"Fuck!" It was pushing Kara over. She was losing her balance. *CRACK!*

The creature's head snapped backward as the vertebrae in its neck fracture. Her hand clenched tightly on its skull, feeling its teeth rip at her sleeve.

The forward motion of the cadaver pushed Kara backward off her feet. She slammed into the frozen ground. The impact caused the creature's head to tear off in Kara's hand. The headless body lay on Kara for what felt like an eternity. Detatched from its head, the corpse became lifeless and limp. Kara pushed it off of her. The skull snapped furiously but harmlessly at her from the end of her arm. Its sickening scream was finally silenced.

Kara stood, still holding the abomination in her hand. Her body began trembling, her nervous system on overload, she glanced in the direction it had attacked her from and saw two more corpses clawing their way out of the river.

"Fuck it!" Kara said. "I'm done."

She couldn't hold off two of them and she knew it. She was going to die. That was reality.

She held up her right hand, complete with snapping zombie head. "I can get one good shot in." She readied herself to smash the severed head into the first zombie's skull.

The first creature stopped dead in its tracks. The second one followed suit. Both immobile, they stared at the severed head in Kara's hand.

Then both turned toward the suddenly deafening sound of distant gunfire, leaving Kara and her new pet.

Looking at the head in her hands, she thought, "Well you might be useful after all."

The cold was beginning to hurt. It wasn't the sharp electric shock that kept rocketing up from Kara's broken left arm. No, this was draining. The cold punished her as she travelled toward the footbridge.

CRACK!

Kara flinched at the sound coming off the snapping head she still clenched. It had snapped at her whenever her hand came within three or four inches of her leg as she ran. But this sound was different—it was far more intense.

"Oh shit!" Kara looking down to see the thing in her hand had just cracked its own jaw with the intensity of its snapping. She held it up to see its lower jaw dangling from its head, like a rooster's comb.

The decapitated fiend tried to snap at her, barely moving its lower mandible.

"You had better still work as a scarecrow you little piece of shit!" Bending down she placed the flesh-covered skull in the snow. The slime from the remnants of its eyeball clung to Kara's thumb as she pulled it silently from the eye socket. Quickly wiping the goop into the snow, she now grabbed her "scarecrow" by its short, scraggly hair.

With a groan Kara got back up. "Not much farther."

She could hear the river. It sounded like it did in spring, during the runoff and the canoe races. She knew she had to move fast. That river was rising, flowing backward. She needed to get across that bridge if she was going to get to her sister.

The barrage of gunfire in the distance behind her gave her comfort. "Keep giving them hell, Jane." She knew her sister's firefight would draw the dead like bees to nectar.

She glanced at the head she grasped tightly. "Just in case, I'll keep you around."

The fiend's never-blinking dead eye burned at her with hatred.

⇒·+⇐

The small throng of five hundred or so dead that had come ashore in front of the convoy vaporized under the thunderous storm of bullets. The frontlines of the huge swarm were no match for the bombardment of molten lead.

"MOVE!!!" Jane screamed to her troops. The dead couldn't stand up to their weaponry, but a far worse foe was rising at them. "THE WATER IS COMING UP FAST!" Water coating the road— only a few inches when Jane first ordered the convoy to pick up the pace—was now nearly a foot deep.

BOOM!

The force of the Humvee to Jane's left smashing into her vehicle was as thunderous as the water tearing away the road beneath her. The rising tide's force had easily lifted the Humvee and crashed it into Jane's vehicle. The force nearly sent Jane airborne, but her death grip on her weapon held her fast in the turret—the machine gun's discharge swerved off her enemy, blasting into the granite mountainside just feet to her right. Razor-sharp shards of rock exploded from the mountainside's face like shrapnel from an anti-personnel mine. A shard sliced Jane's arm with a scalpel's precision; another cut her across the jaw as it flew by, scraping her to the bone, leaving a triangular flap of bloody skin dangling from her jaw. She lurched forward hard, the weapon smashing into her gut, her helmet protecting her head as it bounced off the machine gun mounted to the roof. She felt the wheels grabbing something and looked up to see the other Humvee on its side, water tossing it, dead swarming over it, tearing Sergeant Cornelius to pieces.

CRASH.

Jane's body whiplashed back and forth as her Humvee climbed over the shell of an abandoned Buick, which had been pushed

109

up on them by the wave. The dead car provided traction for the Humvee. Tires suddenly screeched with glee as they clawed pavement. Jane steadied, unleashing her weapon's fury as her vehicle screamed up the rapidly rising incline of the road.

As the remaining vehicles of the convoy climbed the road, Jane screamed on the radio. "Genevieve, patch observation drone footage into my HUD." Only then was Jane able to see the true scope of the horror they were facing.

The wave's speed was slowing dramatically as it reached the center of Westfield. Tons of debris acting as a bulldozer smashed the town. The church spire, the tallest structure in town, snapped and fell as though made of balsa wood instead of brick and timber. As the wave crawled to a stop the inky water frothed at the edge of the new shore just shy of city hall, as corpse after corpse escaped the sea's grasp. Fast dead raced toward the sound of gunfire; slow dead shambled toward the battlefront. Even more dead crawled and oozed their damaged carcasses toward the battle. Missing limbs that were torn from them during the tsunami's pounding, they still moved en masse toward the sound of gunfire. Toward the sound of food.

The corpses streaming and crawling from the muck looked like blood corpuscles flowing through veins. Channels began to form where the fast dead followed one another, trampling their crippled brethren as they rushed to feast. The damaged corpses moved toward the battlefront, as though one large organism lurching toward a meal. To Jane, who was overlooking the battlefield, it seemed like every corpse between Westfield and Manhattan had just washed up on her doorstep. It was far beyond even the most nightmarish of worst-case scenarios the NSA computers had concocted.

Jane's mind calculated; as she watched an uncountable multitude of snarling and screaming corpses emerge from the water, her brain raced over the numbers again and again. As she continued to lay down heavy fire on the enemy racing toward her,

her calculations led to one unacceptable conclusion in her head. Three words that scared her more than anything wouldn't stop tap dancing in her mind.

"Not enough ammo."

—+‹+›—

The sound of the river grew louder as Kara approached a bend in the road that led to the footbridge. She turned her trot into a dash as she smelled the approaching water. Turning the corner she saw the condemned, rusty, iron-framed footbridge.

The water was flowing fast in the wrong direction. It was also rising fast. The water, normally twenty feet below the bridge, was now was lapping at the bottom of it.

Her sister's words flashed in her head: "Quick decisions save lives."

She ran toward the bridge. The chain-link fence gate with a "Bridge Closed" placard attached to it loomed above Kara. She looked at the skull in her hands and tossed it over the fence and onto the rusty grate that still clung to a few rotting wooden slats that formed the walkway. "See you on the other side."

Kara grabbing the steel gate with her right hand and stepped up onto part of the railing that was jutting out from the bridge. It was still too tall—with two hands, it was an easy climb; with one, it was impossible.

Kara began a precarious slide with her feet. While still grasping the fence, she moved her feet to the left as far as she could. She released her hand, and while pushing toward the left, her hand grabbed the icy handrail, swinging her body with the momentum. She shot through the space between handrails and tumbled onto the walkway.

She rose and looked for her decapitated companion. The skull had rolled toward the edge of the bridge. As she made eye contact with it, the thing again tried snapping at her. Lying on its side, the lower jawbone rested against a rusty rivet. The leverage allowed the closed mouth to push open and also pushed the thing off the edge of the bridge. The skull slipped into the rushing water below.

"And then you leave...dead or alive men are all the same."

Kara moved quickly. While climbing through the handrails, she jumped to the rocky former cliff, which was now river bank.

The road rose up on either side of her. She headed toward her left. Back toward the gunfire. Back toward her sister.

POP! POP POP POP!

Kara saw her sister's face every time she heard a shot. She was up ahead. She had to be.

Kara fell to her knees. Exhaustion cut her legs out from under her. Panting hard, the cold hurting her lungs. Not much farther.

The hair on the back of her neck suddenly stood on end. She turned and saw a distant figure running toward her. She got up and ran as fast as she could. The screaming sound it made was drowned out by the gunfire, which echoed deafeningly off the granite canyon that cradled the Westfield River.

"Please be close, sis."

The thing had been just a figure in the distance. Now she could smell it. It was closing in.

Kara knew the gunfire was close, just around the bend. She looked back over her shoulder and saw that the corpse was less than a football field from her.

"Please God, let her be around this corner"

Kara turned the corner and saw the military firing on the dead

"HELP!" Her plea was not audible over the din of screaming corpses and heavy machine-gun fire. "HELP!" she screamed again as she ran.

THUMP!

She went down face-first as the corpse hit her from behind.

The sound of its teeth sinking into her right shoulder and ripping her flesh filled Kara's hearing. Sinew and tendon felt like rubber bands popping in her shoulder. She looked at the corpse as her flesh dangled from his teeth. Its eyes looked at her—pure animal, pure evil, they gleamed with delight as the monster felt a chunk of her flesh slide down its dead gullet.

Time slowed down. Kara knew she was about to die. Eaten alive. And there was nothing she could do about it.

The fiend opened his mouth wide. "This is it." She thought. "This is how I'm going to die." She was astonished at how calm she felt. "It's over." She thought with relief, "At least it's finally over."

BAM!

The zombie's head exploded like a piñata, showering Kara in brain matter, skull fragments, and putrid flesh.

━╬ ╬━

"You've killed all those people," Jane thought. She knew she was going to run out of ammo long before she ran out of enemies. "The camps are sitting ducks. You killed all those people."

"Think!" she screamed at herself as she and her men continued to lay waste to charging hordes of cadavers. "There's got to be a way."

The convoy was closing in on the intersection Jane had chosen for the battle. "You killed all those people."

Jane unleashed a barrage of gunfire. The frontline had stabilized. The mist of her vaporized enemies had created a literal fog of war that had grown so thick that it obscured Jane's vision. The vanguard of the dead's attack were only barely visible as they threw themselves into battle. "NO! There has to be a way!"

Jane's mind, unable to conceive of defeat, grasped for answers. There was no way she was going to lose, not here, not now, and certainly not to an enemy that was basically glorified target practice. "You killed all those people. Those refugee camps will be overrun. You killed all those people."

"Bullshit!" she ferociously replied to her nagging fear.

"Genevieve!"

"Yes ma'am?"

"We are going to change things up. I want everything in the tsunami debris field on fire. Now!"

"Yes ma'am. Heavy airstrikes as well as the drones?"

"Affirmative. Fuel air explosives from the 104th where the debris field meets the open ocean, that's probably around Hartford. I need incendiaries from you starting on the Westfield shore out to Hartford."

"Got it," Genevieve replied.

"Roger that," said the air wing's commander.

"Colonel," Jane barked. "Once the fire is going I'm going to need your men to fly as low and as fast as you can over the inferno. Time to fan the flames."

"Roger that, ma'am. Glad to finally be joining the fight."

"Incendiaries away, ma'am," Genevieve replied.

The convoy firing ferociously at the carrion that pursued them. Racing to their last stand, the intersection of Route 20 and 23, they formed up across the road as they reached it.

"Private, take the turret," Jane said, barking orders at her driver as the vehicle stopped. Jane took her HK MP5-N and leaped out of the Humvee. Empty shell casings from the fifty-caliber guns rained down around her. She rolled underneath one of the Humvees, emerging on the other side next to the turn to Route 23, where her men had positioned the extra weapons and ammo they had secured from the National Guard Armory on Franklin Street. Three DPW dump trucks were filled to the brim with armaments, two fifty-caliber guns, half-a-dozen M-16s, and enough ammo to wipe out a city.

"It's not enough ammo. You failed. They are going to die and it's your fault."

The voice in her head was getting more persistent. "You failed them."

The voice stopped.

The hairs on the back of Jane's neck stood up. Electricity cascaded up and down her spine. Something was behind her.

Jane spun and saw a cadaver tearing a chunk from a victim on the road behind the convoy.

BAM!

A single shot ripped open the top of its skull—the force of the impact sent the dead body reeling off its victim. Jane moved the gun sight onto the woman on the ground. Blood fountained out of her shoulder as if from a ruptured fire hydrant. Jane's eyes locked on the screaming woman. Her blood froze as she realized it was her sister Kara.

Her sister's face contorted with pain and fear. Buckets of blood pumped out of her with every heartbeat. Jane knew she couldn't fail her family again.

"I'm so sorry." She thought, "I can't fail her, I can't let her turn." She pulled the trigger, sending the bullet off, which instantly split her sister's skull in half.

Jane, numb and in shock fell to her knees. Kara's body twitched twice before fully going limp.

Jane didn't hear the din of the distant explosions raining down from the F-15s. Didn't see the glow of the huge fireballs engulfing the horizon or the mushroom clouds billowing into the December sky.

She only saw her sister lying dead in the road. "She was already dead," Jane desperately told herself. "I saved her from becoming one of them."

"Ma'am?"

Jane didn't respond to the radio.

"We need you up here!"

Jane was completely numb. She stood up. Everything in her was gone. She was empty. She felt as dead as her enemy. She turned from her sister's mostly headless carcass and walked slowly back toward the fight.

The air, filled with gunfire and the screams of the dead, erupted in a deafening series of explosions as the jets of the 104th fighter wing broke the sound barrier, buzzing the inferno they had set on top of the tsunami debris field. Behind them the flames exploded in size. What had been a miles wide field of flame reaching hundreds of feet in the air was now becoming a huge spire of flame, reaching thousands of feet in the air. Tornadoes of fire roared to life behind the jets, sucking flaming debris and corpses high into the air. As the jets made pass after pass, the sky became painted in the thick black smoke rising from the sea. The horizon was orange from the F-15 firestorm.

"Die motherfuckers!"

Jane somehow heard the private screaming in delight from the gun turret as he watched the conflagration. "Stop screaming. Keep shooting," she ordered him. "We have a long way to go."

Jane's training took over. Her feelings were gone. She still had a duty to save the rest of these people and her own emotions would not get in the way of that.

The fast dead had momentarily stopped their advance as the world exploded behind them, allowing Jane's forces to open up some breathing room between them and their enemy, vaporizing huge swaths with the fifty-caliber guns. But within moments the throng had decided the convoy was still their main target, and the war was back on.

Jane was calm. She took over the gun turret position from the private and began shooting.

"Dead bodies float," she thought emotionlessly as she paused between firing off barrages. "Everything floating in that debris field is going to burn."

"Anything not burning," she thought as she began squeezing off rounds, "is heading toward me."

CLICK CLICK CLICK.

"Reload!" she belted out almost nonchalantly as a private handed ammo up to her.

"Genevieve," she barked into the radio, "how are the refugee camps looking?"

The radio was silent.

"Genevieve? Do you read me? Over."

No reply.

"I knew you would fail them," a small voice whispered inside Jane's mind.

———

The hideous screech cut through the armored plating of the MRAP like no shrapnel could. Genevieve checked her sidearm. Her laptop was now useless. The velocity of the winds coming off the F-15s had ripped the drones from the skies, hurling them into the huge vortexes of fire that were churning above the Atlantic's new coast. As the gun turret bay door flew open the scream of the dead approaching the camp hit Genevieve's ears like a punch to the face. The smell of rotting flesh kicked her lungs hard as she coughed.

Genevieve pulled her sidearm and shot the first one she saw, a child, no more than seven or eight years old. Its pallid head was torn completely off by the bullet. She felt the second one rushing up on her from her right. A teen girl when it died, this one was racing toward Genevieve with the speed of a cheetah. Its snarling face exploded as a round from Genevieve's gun ended its afterlife.

Genevieve scanned the scene. The camp was under attack. A wave of slow-moving monsters staggered toward the barbed-wire perimeter. She spun around 360 degrees in the turret while scanning for fast-moving targets.

"Only one fast one," she thought. "Makes no sense."

Genevieve's peripheral vision caught movement to her right. While spinning around with her hand firmly grasping the fifty-caliber trigger, she saw two small, terrified children running toward her. Running up from behind them was a small pack of twelve children with pallid flesh and blood-soaked lips in full pursuit.

"Fuck!"

Genevieve couldn't unload the fifty caliber without killing the healthy kids. This war was a numbers game—there was only one key to winning. Lieutenant Commander Kerr's words at the briefing rang in her head. "Save everybody."

Genevieve again went to her sidearm. She shot over the heads of the living children who dove for the ground at the sound of gunshots. The small carcasses of the dead children pursuing them fell as Genevieve's rounds exploded their skulls.

The two children being pursued now lay motionless on the ground between Genevieve and the remains of their attackers. Genevieve looked at the two: one—a girl—huddled over the other, acting as a shield to a younger boy. The children had tears streaming from their eyes as they looked up at Genevieve. The girl's trembling lips formed a single silent word: "HELP."

"Run!" Genevieve screamed. The two children complied and instantly started running toward the MRAP. Genevieve slid down the gun turret into the body of the vehicle. She swung the driverside door open, leaped out of the vehicle, and raced toward the children. The small girl's eyes widened in fear as her body suddenly stopped. The boy stopped screaming as he pointed toward a fast corpse that was gaining on Genevieve.

Drawing her sidearm instinctively, Genevieve screamed, "DOWN!" The two kids dropped instantly to their knees, bending their heads down to the ground and clasping their hands over the back of their heads. Genevieve jumped over the children while spinning and firing two rounds—the first round punctured her undead pursuer in the chest; the second round turned its head inside out. Genevieve hit the ground, rolled, quickly jumped to her feet, and scrambled back to the kids.

"You hurt?"

The girl looked up at her and shook her head no. The boy gasped for air, his terror-filled sobs threatening to choke the life out of him.

"He hurt?"

"No," the young girl replied.

The sound of screaming was suddenly deafening. Genevieve saw a throng of slow dead moving toward them, blocking the way back to the MRAP. Genevieve grabbed the girl by the collar of her shirt and the boy by his belt. She picked the children up and ran toward a century-old maple tree just past the pool of viscera that had been chasing these two kids moments before.

Inside the empty MRAP the radio blared Lieutenant Commander Jane Kerr's voice. "Genevieve. How are the refugee camps looking? Genevieve? Do you read me? Over."

⭐

Jane and her crew—coated in burned gun lube and a thin sheen of human flesh from the horde—were now using old M-16's, the fifty caliber guns having melted from hours of continuous firing.

"You never saw the face of the thing on top of Kara," she thought. "Could've been Michael."

"Yeah, I know." Despair filled Jane as she realized she was right. She probably killed both of her siblings.

"Too late for both them…again." Jane wiped the sticky film of dead human, obscuring her vision, from her goggles.

She had failed her family. Her position would be overrun within the hour. No word from Genevieve or any of the other refugee camps.

"Failure," she thought.

Bam bam click click click.

"OUT!" Jane screamed into the microphone while throwing the empty ammunition drum backward. A soldier below threw Jane a new fully loaded drum—Jane snapped it back into place. *Bam bam bam.*

"OUT!" another soldier screamed.

"That's it," a voice responded. "Last drum."

"Bayonets ready," Jane barked. "This shit is going to be up close and personal."

Jane braced for the onslaught. The fog was so dense with the flesh of the dead it was blinding. Visions of Kara flickered in her thoughts: vacations in Ocean Park, birthday parties, and happy times—the ones you don't even realize are the most precious and important of your lives, until death is upon you.

Jane's muscles tightened. "Where are they?" The screaming hadn't subsided, but the dead still hadn't attacked.

Gusts of wind began rolling down the Berkshires, a sure sign of a coming storm. The fog of war began settling out. The enemy forces came into focus. "They're slow!" an ecstatic soldier screamed.

Jane clenched her teeth. She became aware of the wound to her jaw for the first time as the flap of skin that was still clinging to her face brushed against her neck. Jane snatched the piece of skin, ripped it from her face, and threw it down without a glance or a second thought.

The order to charge almost escaped her lips, but she faintly heard something through the shrieks of the carcasses that were closing in on her that caused her to pause.

BOOM!

The fifty-foot-tall pine tree landed like a bomb on the road between Jane and her final foes.

"Chainsaw!" Jane knew she had heard something. Looking up, she saw them. Civilians lined the granite ridge above them.

BOOM! BOOM!

Two more trees fell, forming a wall between Jane's forces and her enemy. Two more trees were about to fall as men with chainsaws sliced through the wood. Next to the lumberjacks were rows of people with shotguns and handguns who were firing down into the zombie horde.

The hair on Jane's neck suddenly shot to attention. She turned ready to fire, sure the enemy was moving fast on her flank. The crowd surging toward her was screaming for battle, and to Jane's astonishment, they were alive. Nearly a hundred strong, the living were not going to go quietly into the great beyond. Carrying bats, axes, and every conceivable form of handheld weaponry both blunt and sharp, they charged. "Boys," Jane quipped on the radio, "I think the cavalry just arrived."

———⊰+⊱———

Blood splashed up from Genevieve's feet as she dashed through the remains of the pack of dead children.

"CLIMB!" she shouted at the two children as they reached the tree. She swung the young girl up with her left hand—who hit a low-lying branch hard. Instead of instantly scrambling up, she looked down, extended her arm, and screamed "Foley!" to the small boy, who had been flung over Genevieve's shoulder, and was now airborne Foley hit the thick branch with a thud. The young girl grabbed the boy by the shirt as he hit the tree. They both quickly glanced down at the soldier who had saved them.

"FUCKING CLIMB!!!"

Genevieve's snarling face seemed no different to the kids than the faces sported by the dead. Both children began scrambling up the ancient maple tree. Neither looked back down at their rescuer.

Genevieve drew her weapon as she turned to face the herd. They were everywhere. Three gunshots rang out from somewhere in the camp. The undead paused and their screaming momentarily let up. While looking for the source of the sounds, Genevieve turned and scrambled up the tree—there was a time to fight and a time to hide...this was the latter.

More gunshots rang through the camp as Genevieve raced up the tree. She knew the weaponry that was being used simply by hearing it. There was at least one .22 caliber handgun, a shotgun, and two hunting rifles being used, but she couldn't get a fix on where the shots were coming from. She looked up and saw the two kids clinging to each other and the tree about ten feet above her position, which was almost twenty feet up. She caught their eye, put her finger to her lips, and mouthed "SHHHH" to them just as the dead resumed their horrifying war cry.

"How did this go so bad so quickly?" she thought. "Why didn't anyone put up a fight?"

The gunshots seemed to be coming from the far edge of the camp. Many of the dead were moving in that direction, but not all. Several dozen surrounded the base of the maple tree that Genevieve and the children were trapped in and dozens more shambled between the tree and the MRAP.

Genevieve looked up again at the kids and then climbed up to meet them. "It's OK," she said as she got closer. "They can't climb."

The girl's look conveyed her doubt and disbelief without saying a word.

"I fought these things before," she said, reassuring the two. "They can't climb." She continued: "I'm Sergeant Genevieve. April Genevieve."

"I'm Foley," the little boy blurted out.

"Hi Foley," Genevieve said and then looked to the girl. "And you?"

"Jaime," the girl answered.

"You guys brother and sister?"

The two simultaneously replied, "No."

The boy's eyes widened. He began to tremble.

Genevieve looked down and saw one very determined carcass clawing at the tree bark. Its fingers snapped as a result of the intensity of its effort.

"It's OK. It's dumb," she said up to the frightened kids. "Look, it can't climb, Foley. You are better than it is."

"I'm better, too," Jamie replied.

"Yeah you are," Genevieve answered, her voice reassuring and confident. "So much better than them it's ridiculous. That's why you're alive."

Foley started sobbing. "I'm...sniff...not better...sniff...than mommy. Why...why is she..."

"My mommy and daddy are dead, too," Genevieve replied. "It's not fair, but it happens to all of us."

"You too?" Foley asked in a voice filled that was equal parts terror and sorrow.

"Me too," Genevieve said. "But you know who is still alive? My grandma...and I guarantee you she will save us."

"I never had a grandma," Jamie replied. Foley stared at Genevieve—his eyes filled with tears.

"Well let me tell you.. Once she saves us she can be your grandma, too."

The gunshots in the camp were less aggressive. Less numerous. "Either they are dying, or they are retreating," Genevieve thought before reengaging the two terrified kids.

"You might have seen her," she continued, trying to keep the kids calm. "She was on TV. Dressed like me, but she has silver hair."

"And...and the word 'grandma' written on her hat?" Jaime asked. Her voice was trembling.

"We call it a helmet, Jaime, but yes, that was her."

"She was scary," Foley blurted out, his little brow furrowed.

"Yes. Yes she is," Genevieve confirmed with a smile. "That's why she is going to win this and come rescue us."

The two kids looked at each other for reassurance.

Genevieve checked her sidearm. Three rounds left. Enough to take care of the kids and herself, just in case.

"It's OK, Foley," Jaime assured the small boy. "Grandma is going to save us."

�====+ +⟩====

The road was covered in a sticky paste, byproduct of the remnants of flesh-colored fog settling. The paste actually provided excellent footing for the humans as they ran toward the dead.

The first few corpses had made it over the huge trees that stood between them and their prey when the human front line smashed into them. The humans were brutally efficient as they smashed, stabbed, and sliced the corpses back to death. The dead couldn't hold a candle to the brutality of the living. Humans had watched their world die on television and their loved ones die beside them. Now it was payback time.

The creatures, slow but vicious, were no match for blade and baseball bat. Devoid of their fast brethren, the slow dead fell quickly.

The screams of the dead were mingled with the war screams of the living. Names of loved ones who had fallen mixed with primal screaming and obscenities. Frustration and fear had become ferocity. They tore into the undead just as viciously as the corpses had attacked the humans across the globe.

Taking shifts on the front line, the humans hacked and smashed until their arms felt like tree trunks filled with lead. Once exhausted, a human would retreat, giving a rested human its chance for vengeance.

They slogged through the dead advances for hours, eventually fighting on top of corpses in front of the pine tree barricade. Hours of carnage and brutality finally paid off.

BOOM BOOM.

Trees began falling again from the ridgeline, only this time they were on fire, and they were falling behind enemy lines. The dead caught between the first flaming tree and the human front lines didn't last long. The flames, being the only thing the dead were afraid of, sent the corpses into a frenzy—some veered off their warpath and plunged off the side of Route 20 and down the steep and sharp granite cliff face into the river below. Others just shambled from the flames straight into the human lines and were destroyed with vicious efficiency by the living.

Once the dead's front lines had been dispatched, the humans scrambled quickly back past the military convoy.

Jane watched as the ridgeline above began raining down metal containers.

"Everybody down!" a civilian voice screamed behind Jane.

Jane, having recognized the metal containers for what they were—propane tanks from backyard grills—dove for cover. The propane tanks rained down on top of the hundreds of remaining corpses and on top of the flaming trees. The heat and flame quickly igniting the gas inside—explosions tore through the dead as though they were made of tissue paper. *BOOM BOOM BOOM.*

And then it was quiet.

A husky, bearded man holding up a bloody axe stood and began screaming—a wild, uncontrollable scream unlike any that had been heard on that day. He was screaming for joy, for life, for victory. His scream spread like an infection through the human ranks. Boisterous screams rose from the victors as they hugged one another. Some had tears of joy; some had tears of grief and sorrow for their loved ones who had fallen.

Jane sat down—she was exhausted and numb. There was a thin film of dead flesh on her and everything around her. She did not cheer and she did not cry. She sat wishing she could feel something, but glad that she wasn't. Her dead sister, and what she believed was the carcass of her dead brother, lay a few hundred yards away. "Numb is good," she thought.

"There she is!!!" the bearded man said while rushing over to Jane. "Thank you!" he bellowed as he came up on her. Jane stood. The man's eyes, still crazed with the energy of war, were as wide as saucers. "Thank you!" He said as he bear hugged the emotionally dead woman. Before he had released his grasp the entire throng of humans was around Jane, some crying, some cheering, all of them adoring her.

Jane felt sick to her stomach. Each "thank you" and each hug pushed her closer to vomiting.

"I didn't save them," she thought. "They saved themselves."

"What did I do?" Her inner dialogue continued: "I killed my family and almost killed everyone else because I didn't have enough ammo."

"We love you," a fanatical voice screamed out, followed by another round of cheering from the crowd.

Jane, needing to stop this, held up her hand in a gesture to silence the undeserved adulation. "I lost contact with the camps. How were they when you left?" she asked the bearded man.

"We weren't in the camps," the bearded man replied. "We're from the hill towns. We watched you on TV and knew where you were going to fight. We wanted to go out swinging, but you..." A huge grin crossed his face. "You saved us." A cheer broke out again.

Jane, unimpressed, put up both hands. "Stop."

The crowd hushed.

"None of you are from the camps."

"No," an exhausted woman replied. "In every zombie movie the refugee camps are always death traps..."

"Mount up!" Jane barked to her men, cutting off the woman. The soldiers quickly scrambled into their Humvees. Jane pushes past her fans and moved toward her vehicle. Entering her vehicle, she quickly popped open the gun turret and emerged out of it.

Without waiting for the civilians to ask, she simply yelled at the top of her lungs, "We still have people to save!" She hit the top of the war machine twice signaling her driver to take off. The cheers arising from the humans faded quickly as the convoy sped up Route 23 toward the camps. Jane, deaf to the fanfare, kept hearing two words over and over again in her head: "Death traps."

—◄+ +►—

"She's alive!" Jane shouted as she saw Sergeant Genevieve and her two tiny companions halfway up the leafless maple tree. Turning to the private driving, she ordered, "Plow the road!"

The private hit the gas—a few hundred undead bodies, no matter how motivated, could never hope to stand against an armored Humvee. Jane opened her door. Bracing herself in the doorjamb while forcing the heavy reinforced steel door open as wide as possible, she said, "Everyone follow my lead. Make the plow bigger."

SPLAT! The first of many corpses exploded on the other side of the door from Jane, followed fast by another and another. The impact from the barrage of dead plowing into her was horrendous—every hit racked her body with pain as the dead exploded only inches from her on the other side of the door. "Take it!!!" she berated herself. "Take it!!! You deserve pain!!!" Every hit now sounded to Jane like a gunshot, every creature crushed now the sound of her sister's head exploding. More and more lurid details from that moment leaked into her mind's eye. Jane punished herself with each and every impact as the Humvees were crushing the dead under their wheels..

127

The vehicle slowed to a halt and the impacts stopped. Jane, covered in the filth of the undead, moved her stiffened muscles slowly as she left the doorjamb. She stood in front of the maple tree. Sergeant Genevieve stood below it, by the trunk, saluting her.

"What happened here..." Jane said, but before she could finish her sentence she was hit hard in the legs by two squealing children.

"Grandma, we knew you'd come. We knew you would," Jaime shouted.

Foley was sobbing. While holding Jane's leg and looking up at her. Through tears of joy, he kept saying, "I love you, Grandma...I love you, Grandma."

ACT 3
REVELATIONS

FIFTEEN YEARS LATER...

"The next few hours brought incredible news," Foley said—his voice brimmed with pride as he read from his speech. "The 104th pilots spread the word to forces up and down the East Coast to set the debris field on fire. And it worked." Foley felt Jaime rubbing his shoulders, soothing him while he read. "Air force units coordinated incendiary strikes and supersonic flyovers to superb effect."

"While some camps fell," Foley said and glanced up from his notes to look at his audience of one. The old woman somberly stared at the dirt path they all stood on. Foley continued: "Most camps made it through unscathed. Survivors quickly became heroes, people of all ages, religions, and creeds came together. They organized search-and-rescue missions. They fought the undead through cities and suburbs, rescuing thousands who were unable to evacuate and had been going at it alone." Foley was so proud of the woman he had always called Grandma and said, "Lieutenant Commander Jane Kerr saved us on that day. She showed us the true meaning of sacrifice and bravery. Without her inspiration and leadership that day none of us would be here." He looked up at Grandma, hoping she was enjoying his speech. "We all literally owe her our lives." Jaime gave a small, loving squeeze to the back of Foley's neck as he finished.

"So what do you think?" Foley asked.

The old warrior looked up from the ground, tears welling in her eyes, and said, "I think…" Her voice was as withered as her sixty-one-year-old body. "I think it fucking sucks!"

"Really!" Jaime snapped at the furious old woman. "Can't you ever be nice?"

"What's there to be nice about?" the old woman asked and spit on the dirt path. "You forgot the part about how the whole East Coast burned."

"We didn't burn," Foley replied. "We're still here."

"Yeah, because of snow!" Grandma snapped. "Not because of me! Because there was a snowpack in the Northeast the fires stayed offshore up here. But nowhere else. Because of me the whole East Coast of the United States burned. I killed millions of people!"

"Infected people," Jaime said, trying to comfort her.

"I didn't save shit!"

"OK," Foley said. "Forget it, I have a different version of the speech."

Grandma looked wearily at him.

"It's about the first person who didn't change. The old lady, who died three days after the battle, remembering the feeling of joy we all felt when she didn't turn, knowing the infection had stopped."

"Don't forget the feeling of radiation poisoning we all have now," Grandma replied sarcastically.

"You know, I'm sorry you don't believe you're a hero!" Jaime, sick of having this argument again, snapped. "But you are! You saved every last living person on Earth. Without you every one of us would have died!"

"Jaime, please..." Foley said. "Remember, the doctor said for you to stay calm." He glanced down at her very pregnant belly.

She shot a look at Foley that told him to shut up.

"The people of this world need a hero and like it or not that's you, Grandma."

"Grandma, it's been fifteen years. They just want to honor you," Foley said, interrupting his wife while avoiding the death stare Jaime was now giving him.

Lieutenant Commander Jane Kerr looked hard at the two people in front of her. She had spent the last fifteen years of her life raising them. Foley, now a twenty-one-year-old man, stood beside Jaime, his twenty-two-year-old wife who was only a few days away from delivering their first child. They both had been such a Godsend to her. These two kids had been the only things that had kept Jane from eating a gun, and as they stood there, Jane still couldn't believe just how stupid they were acting.

"Honor me?" Jane replied, her tone filled with disgust. "That's bullshit!"

"But you saved us," Jaime said, hoping there was still a tiny spark of sanity left in the woman she and Foley lovingly referred to as Grandma. "You saved us all."

The sixty-one-year-old warrior sneered, "How stupid are you?"

Jaime took a deep breath, the way she always did when Grandma would get "confused," and said, "Without you the world would've died. Without you..." She paused and placed her hands over her very pregnant belly. "Without you this baby..."

"Oh shut the fuck up!" Jane said and spat on the dirt path the three were now walking on. "I need a fucking drink."

Jane's age, alcoholism, and radiation poisoning had taken a toll on her. "Where's my fucking flask?" she asked. Her wrinkled hands started searching her pockets.

"You left it back at the house," Foley responded.

"Then I'm going back to the fucking house." Jane turned and began walking away from the couple.

"Please," Jaime begged, "don't be like this."

Jane stopped, turned around, and snapped, "Like what?" The withered old woman's eyes caught on fire as fury began building in her. "Answer me! Like what?"

"She didn't mean anything…"

"Shut up Foley! Your wife is a big girl. She can speak for herself!"

"I just meant—" Jaime began to explain when Grandma cut her off.

"You just meant. You just meant." Grandma's eyes shot knives at Jaime. "You just meant stop acting like a crazy woman."

"No, I really didn't."

"A crazy woman," Grandma continued over Jaime's protest. "I'm crazy. Isn't that what you all say behind my back?" The old woman spat on the ground again. "You all think the world is safe. IT'S NOT!" Her eyes darted back and forth between the two, her volume increasing with every sentence. "The world is not safe. And I saved nothing!"

"You saved us!" Jaime screamed back, shocking Grandma into silence. "You saved us. Without you we'd be dead. This child would never be born. Like it or not, you are a hero."

"Hero? There were close to eight billion people living over this entire planet. Now how many are there? Less than a twenty thousand clinging to life on this old mountain range turned archipelago."

SCREEE SCREEE SCREEE.

A black squirrel ran out across the path from the underbrush, his cry one of pure terror as he raced up a nearby tree. Jaime and Foley froze as they heard the clickety-clack of a two-foot-long centipede racing after its prey. The large black carnivorous bug darted across the road, quickly scrambling up the tree, and grasped the squirrel's leg in its mandibles. The rodent screamed in agony as the centipede began consuming it.

THUNK!

A knife streaked like lightning toward the carnage, splitting the squirrel's head in two, killing it instantly. The centipede was too busy eating to notice.

"Why don't you ever kill the bug, Grandma?" Jaime turned to ask the old woman, her arm still extended from throwing the knife.

" 'Cause the squirrel was already dead," Grandma said, turned away from the couple, and began walking home. "Besides, bugs need to eat, too. It's called the circle of life."

"Just going to leave your knife?" Foley asked.

"Yep. I'll come back when it's done eating."

"What about the ceremony? The unveiling of your statue?" Foley shouted to the old woman who was walking away from him.

Without looking back, the sixty-one-year-old woman held up her fist and extended her middle finger.

⊨┼ ┼⊨

"Why is she so difficult!" Foley fumed. "Why?!?"

"She remembers how it used to be," Jaime replied.

"Well so do I and I don't act like that," Foley snapped in frustration.

"You were six and I was seven. She remembers a whole lot more than we ever could."

"I'm not so sure, some of her stories are pretty crazy," Foley responded.

"She is the oldest person alive in the world," Jaime answered. "Of course she's crazy. But that doesn't mean she doesn't remember."

"Really?" Foley asked and started smiling while thinking of all the wild and crazy stories Grandma had told them growing up. "Remember the sky telescopes? What did she call them?"

"Satellites," Jaime responded. A grin began to cross her lips.

"Yeah, satellites." Foley laughed. " I loved that story. Telescopes floating in the sky pointed at the ground so people could see what was going on."

Jaime giggled. "That one was nuts, got to admit it." She rolled her eyes. "Oh Grandma, why did you have to go crazy?"

"Ooh, how about monkeys?"

Jaime laughed so hard at the thought of little hairy people with tails swinging through the trees that she started snorting. "And what was that thing they ate?"

"Bananas!"

They both completely lost it. Jaime was laughing so hard that she worried the baby might pop out right then and there.

"So," Foley said while trying to catch his breath. "What about tomorrow?"

"We tell the president she's sick. There's a touch of the cough going around," Jaime said and smiled.

"Think they'll believe it?"

"It's up to us to protect her legacy," Jaime stated. "People don't want their heroes to have problems. Heroes have to be perfect."

"Perfectly crazy."

"Well we've known that for years, Foley," Jaime said and looked at her husband with absolute love in her eyes. "It's why we are still the only ones who know she's nuts."

"I think people just don't want to know."

"Possibly. But whatever, we should start back soon, make sure she's OK."

"She went home to get drunk. It's the only time she ever seems OK."

"You're right. No need to rush home." Jaime kissed Foley on the cheek.

"You are so beautiful." Foley smiled from the peck on the cheek. "I mean it, too. You are really gorgeous."

"Thanks," Jaime responded. "You don't think I look fat in these pants?"

"You're nine months pregnant, babe," he said. "You look fat no matter what pants you're wearing." He smiled at her.

"Well at least the man I love has the smallest penis on Earth." She smiled. "I mean next to you of course—your dick is way tiny, too."

They both broke out laughing again.

───※ ※───

Jaime and Foley gave Grandma a good half hour of drinking time before they headed back from their walk. They hoped she would be more pleasant as the grain alcohol swept away her sobriety.

"Oh no! No. No. No. No." Foley felt his heart drop.

"What?" Jaime replied.

"Look." Her husband pointed in the direction the house they shared with Grandma. Above the tree line orange smoke was rising. "Zombie smoke." His voice was filled with utter despair. "She lit the zombie smoke."

"Oh god, not again." Jaime replied. "How long do you think this one will last?"

"Last time she had an episode, it lasted almost a week."

"Well at least we won't be lying tomorrow when we say she's too sick to attend the ceremony."

"We? One of us is going to have to stay with her. We can't leave her when she's like this."

"I know." Jaime thought back on the last time Grandma had an episode. An entire week with the old lady on the roof with her sniper rifle, screaming, "They're back! They're back!" every time a twig snapped or a breeze moved a tree branch.

"Well there is always an upside," Foley said with a grin. "Last time she shot every centipede that she saw."

"I really wish bugs were still small," Jaime replied.

"I really wish Grandma would get better," Foley answered.

"Me too."

⚔ ⚔

"What the fuck is wrong with the two of you?!" Grandma was running down the driveway toward her family, sniper rifle slung over her shoulder. "Can't you see the smoke? They're back! They're back!"

"Grandma," Foley said. His voice was cautious as he spoke. "Do you remember the last time...they were back?"

"Don't you dare take that tone with me boy!" Grandma snapped back. The smell of homemade alcohol wafting from her was thick in the air. "Foley, go check the arsenal, make sure everything is still loaded. Jaime, go check the vehicle, make sure we have enough food and fuel in case this shit goes sideways and we have to bug out."

"I check the vehicle every night. Just like Foley checks the arsenal every night..."

"God damn it, don't patronize me!" Grandma's voice cracked like a whip. "Go inside you two smart-asses! Look at the news and then tell me how crazy I am."

Jaime and Foley looked at each other and raised their eyebrows. "That's what you said last time..."

"JUST GO LOOK!"

Foley and Jaime had hoped to reason with her—it had worked once to bring her back to reality. But not this time. The drunken little old lady, veins bulging in her temples, looked as though she might have a stroke if she got any more upset.

"Well let's go see how bad it is," Jaime said. Foley, smiling, nodded in agreement.

⊱⊰

"Reports are coming in from all over the nation of outbreaks." The newscaster's voice greeted the couple as they entered the house, and the images on screen confirmed the worst.

Foley stopped breathing. Cold shards of electricity shot down his spine. His skin turned to gooseflesh. It had taken fifteen years to forget. And in less than fifteen seconds, it was all back. All the memories he had killed came roaring back to life.

He was six, running down the hallway of his house toward his baby sister's room. The door flew open. "No!!!" he shrieked. The cry rang out in his memory, echoing in his ears.

His mother's dead eyes were locked on him. Blood and brain matter dripped from her chin. His 10 month old baby sister's body was limp in mom's hands. Most of his sister's tiny head had been gnawed away.

"Foley!!!"

It was his brother's voice. Suddenly he was being lifted. Thrown over his big brother's shoulders. He saw her for the last time, staggering toward them, her arms reaching out as she began that hideous scream.

"No!!!"

"That's not mommy anymore," his brother Jaden said as he ran out of the house.

"We're heading toward the camps," Jaden said as he ran down the yard. "We'll be safe there."

"Foley!"

Grandma's voice hit his ears as hard as her hand hit the back of his head. "Snap out of it!"

"Sorry." He was back in the living room, covered in cold sweat, trembling like a leaf before a storm.

The newscaster's voice continued over scenes of carnage. "Authorities are urging the public to stay calm…"

"Fuck calm," Grandma drunkenly replied. "Fuck the authorities."

"Grandma, please," Jaime said.

"Didn't you see the smoke?"

"We saw the orange smoke," Jaime said.

Frustration etched across her face, the old warrior replied, "No, that's the signal. The orange soot is the signal." She walked to the front door and opened it while looking back at Jaime. "I said the smoke."

Jaime quickly moved to Grandma's side and said, "Oh God."

Thick black smoke was rising from the south. "We didn't see it…the forest, the trees are so thick…we didn't."

"Get in here!" Foley said. His voice was shrill with fear.

Jaime and Grandma looked at him pointing at the screen. He turned to them, eyes filled with tears. Jaime hadn't seen that look on her only love's face since they were kids. She rushed to him.

"It's Noble!" His body wanted to implode as he spoke. "It's Noble Hospital!"

Jaime embracing him quickly, cooing, "Shhh…" Glancing to the TV as she cradled him, she saw Noble Hospital, which was to the south of them, engulfed in flames. Military police were surrounding it, weapons at the ready.

"Foley!" Grandma's whiskey-soaked voice roared. He looked at her while still being embraced by Jaime. "Come here."

Jaime, still cuddling her traumatized husband, looked back at Grandma. The old woman's arms were outstretched. Jaime let go of Foley.

Grandma's outstretched hands grasped Foley by his shoulders—her arms were locked and she snapped Foley's body more upright. "We," she said. Her voice was calm. "Look at me in the eyes, boy."

Foley looked at her. Her eyes were bright and lucid in a way he hadn't seen since he was a child.

"Good." She continued: "Believe me. We will get out of this. I have a plan for every contingency." She glanced at her adopted daughter, then looked back at Foley. "We have to keep her safe." Foley nodded silently.

"And I need you back. I need you to be here and now." She could feel his body trembling less and less as she spoke. "I have a plan. I have a safe place where we can ride out the storm. But I need you to put all your personal shit aside and help me get your wife and your baby to safety."

"Wife and baby." Foley repeated the words in his mind, and he snapped back to the present. Every fear drained from his body as fast as they had strangled him. He took a deep, grounding breath. His jaw muscles tightened. "What's the plan?" he asked.

Grandma's face beamed with pride. "That's my boy," she said while tussling his hair.

"OK," Jaime interjected. "Really, what's the plan?" Pain etched across her face as she spoke.

Grandma looked at her adopted daughter, who was standing in a puddle of amniotic fluid. "Your water broke," she said.

"No kidding!" Jaime said. Fear, sarcasm, and mind-numbing pain flavored her response. "What's the fucking plan?"

"We're going to Tekoa," Grandma replied. "We are going to see the doctor."

⚔ ⚔

Foley thought it made perfect sense. The doctor was amazing. He remembered her showing up at the camp months after the war. People were dying from a new disease, and then the doctor limped into camp, appearing out of nowhere with a cure. She was brilliant. She was the woman who taught people how to be doctors and nurses again.

"Foley," Grandma said. "Here and now."

"Right," he replied. "What do you need me to do?"

"There are extra MREs upstairs, get them. Jaime and I will get the car ready. Meet us outside with the supplies."

"Got it," Foley replied as he darted up the stairs.

"Now," Grandma said and turned to Jaime, "let's get you to the car."

Jaime nodded. The pain from another contraction prevented her from responding. Grandma put Jaime's arm over her shoulder and quickly lead her toward their car.

⊷⊶

"Where are you?" Foley wanted to stay calm as he began searching the storage. "Where the hell did you put the MREs?" Searching quickly gave way to ransacking as seconds ticked by.

"Gotcha!" euphoria cascaded over every pore of his body as he found two boxes filled with meals ready to eat. The boxes were bulky, but light—he moved them toward the door.

BAM BAM.

Foley dropped the boxes at the sound of gunfire. Racing to the window, he saw a green pickup truck moving up the road, toward the house. Two men with guns were standing in the back firing at a slow-moving herd of zombies pursuing them. "You fucking idiots!" Foleys heart thumped in his chest. "You're bringing them toward us!" Foley turned from the parade of corpses staggering up the dirt road to their home. While grabbing the boxes, he darted into the hallway in the direction of the stairwell. Carrying his cargo, one stacked on top of the other, he began descending the stairs. On the third step down his left foot tripped his right.

CRACK! The sound of his shoulder separating as he hit the floor boomed like thunder. He experienced mind-numbing pain and heard gunshots. "Jaime!" he thought. Pain didn't matter to Foley or fear or anything other than his wife. She was everything to him, and she needed him. His baby needed him. Foley stood. The pain in his shoulder felt as though a flaming axe was stuck in his flesh. His head cleared, and Foley staggered toward the front door.

———

"Lie down in the back." Grandma eased Jaime into the back of the aging Humvee. "I'll go get Foley and…" *BAM BAM.*

"Two rounds, from two weapons, both shotguns, coming from the road, probably a half mile or less from here." Grandma's mind was as much a finely honed weapon of war as her body.

"Suicide squads?" Jaime replied.

Grandma hadn't realized she had said her situational assessment out loud. "Probably," she responded. "Just lie down. I'm pulling the car out front—we'll be safe at the doctor's and before you know it you and Foley are going to have a brand new bouncing baby."

"Just get Foley and let's go!" Another contraction clamped around her body like a vice—they were coming too fast. Jaime knew something was wrong. "It'll be OK. It'll be fine," she thought as another contraction tore at her.

Grandma roared the Humvee to life and pulled out in front of the house. The suicide squad was in sight. A green pickup, rust eating holes in its body. Two fools stood in the flatbed—the kickback from each round fired off threatened to send them tumbling out of the truck. "Fuckin' amateurs," Grandma grumbled as she saw them approach. Leaning out the car window, she yelled, "Foley! Let's go!"

Grandma saw the door swing open. Foley's face was racked with pain—his nose was broken, his face was thickly covered in blood, and his left arm was so twisted that his hand faced backward. Grandma looked at him, he had the same look she saw that day when he ran into her arms at the camp. A look of pure... *BAM!*

Foley's chest cavity exploded in blood as he fell back. Grandma turned around to see the driver of the pickup pointing a smoking handheld weapon at them. The two men in the flatbed waved at her, beckoning her to join them.

"Foley!" Jaime screamed as she saw her husband fall. She looked to Grandma—the old woman was already standing in front of the vehicle and blasting off a barrage of return fire from her old HK MP5-N. The truck was shredded under the torrent of lead. The driver slumped dead over the wheel, flipping the pickup on its side. The two flatbed passengers flew from the truck, their bodies crumpling with the sickening crack of bones breaking as they slammed to the ground.

Jaime turned from the carnage in front of her to the horror behind her. "Foley!" Her scream was filled with pure joy. Grandma whirled around. Foley was standing on the porch. His left shoulder and his arm were broken, part of his chest cavity was missing.

Grandma jumped in the vehicle, locked the doors, and took off.

"Wait! What are you doing?" Jaime pleaded as they tore across the front lawn and onto the street toward Shelbi's and away from her only true love. "You crazy fucking cunt! Turn around—he's alive!"

Grandma turned to face the woman she had raised from childhood. "No."

Jaime ignored the pain of a searing contraction and reached for the steering wheel. A quick backhanded fist from Grandma to Jaime's jaw knocked her unconscious.

Grandma's mind focused on saving those she could: Jaime and her unborn child.

⟞⟜ ⟞⟜

"Foley, let's go!"

Staggering toward the door, he wanted to scream out for help. But he wasn't important right now. Only his family mattered. "Get to the car," he thought. "The doctor can fix you up after the baby's OK." Everything hurt. With every step he took pain shot up and down his spine. Turning the doorknob was an excruciating ordeal. The door swung open and he took a step out onto the porch. He saw Grandma and was suddenly hit in the chest with the force of a Mack truck, sending him flying backward.

"Oh my God! I've been shot." Foley went numb. "It's shock, you're in shock. Get up, get to Grandma." His memory darted back to a story she'd told him about saving a guy in Venezuela once. He was shot three times and she carried him out of the jungle on her back. "Get up!" His body tingled as if massive amounts of Novocain were flowing through his bloodstream. He couldn't feel himself getting up. "Just shock. You're in shock."

Now standing, Foley looked at Grandma, who was standing next to the Humvee, machine gun smoking in her hand and tears streaming down her face. "Tears?!" The sight shocked Foley. She got in the car and drove away.

Foley could not believe his eyes. "She left me."

SNAP!

The sound of a branch snapping sounded unbelievably loud. Foley looked down and saw his death approaching. A corpse was staggering up the steps toward him. Foley didn't move—he didn't want to. His family had left him. He was abandoned, alone. The creature stepped onto the porch, its mouth slightly open in a permanent snarl.

145

"This is it," he thought, too terrified to flee. "This is how I'm going to die."

And then it happened. The creature walked right by him. "Oh no." Foley knew he was infected. He knew in every fiber of his being what was happening, the radiation had stopped working. "No." But he wouldn't accept it. "No." He tried to move, nothing happened. "Oh my god." Panic filled his soul. "I'm not breathing! I'M NOT BREATHING!"

BAM!

One of the men who had been thrown from the truck and was lying on the ground had pulled out a sidearm. He was shooting at the approaching herd. The zombies let out their horrifying scream. Foley hated that sound, the sound that had haunted his nightmares his whole life. He heard it differently than before. He finally heard it correctly for the first time. The screaming of the corpses was so simple. "Why can't they understand?"

Foley saw his body begin to move toward the wounded man. Foley began to open his mouth. The sound that had terrified him as a child poured from him as loudly as he could manage. "KILL ME!" his voice screamed, joining with the hideous chorus. "PLEASE! KILL ME!"

<hr/>

Grandma turned the vehicle hard down the dirt road to the doctor's. "We are almost here." She wanted her voice to sound comforting to her daughter. "Your baby is going to be fine."

Jaime lay on the floor of the Humvee unconscious and unresponsive to Grandma's nervous patter.

The doctor's house was now in sight down the dirt road. "There she is!" Grandma exclaimed upon seeing the woman who she had credited with saving humanity standing on the porch.

Everyone always wanted to give the glory for saving the world to her, Lieutenant Commander Jane Kerr. But to her, the woman everyone now called Grandma, the real hero was the doctor, the woman who saved medicine, the person who had actually saved people.

"This is the safest place in the world for you and the baby right now," Grandma said to her unconscious daughter. The Humvee spewed up rocks from its tires as Grandma slammed on the brakes next to the porch that the doctor was standing on.

"She's in labor and Foley's dead!" Grandma barked out the window. "I need your help!"

The woman on the porch moved quickly to the vehicle. She opened the door and saw Jaime semiconscious and lying in a pool of blood. "She's starting to hemorrhage." The doctor said. "Help me move her inside!"

The two women started taking Jaime out of the vehicle.

"Wh...what's..."

"Shhh," Grandma replied to a semi-awake Jaime.

"No, the baby...the..."

"It's OK. We're here with the doctor."

Jaime looked over groggily at the other woman. Waves of relief washed over her upon seeing the kind but worried face of the doctor.

"Shelbi...thank God." Her lips formed a smile as she slipped from consciousness altogether, secure in the thought that she and her baby were safe.

⟞⟝ ⟞⟝

BAM! BAM!

"Oh god please don't run out of bullets." Foley was almost upon the man lying on the ground. "Turn toward me! Shoot me!" The man on the ground had been firing at the horde that had been following them, oblivious to Foley's approach from behind him.

"Shoot me!" The sound echoing from his open chest cavity hurt a lot. His body rattled like a rusty pickup truck hitting the rumble strip built into the roads to wake sleeping drivers up. "Shoot me!"

The man on the ground looked over toward Foley. He raised his gun and aimed it at Foley's face.

"Thank god."

CLICK...

He couldn't believe it. He was so sure he'd be dead. Really dead. The man on the ground began screaming as Foley staggered closer.

"Oh my god no! No! I won't!" Foley's mind began screaming at his unresponsive body. "STOP!" He was almost on top of the man whose screams had morphed into uncontrollable sobbing.

"BRAINS." The horde hissed, the scream of "KILL ME" gone, now replaced with "BRAINS."

Foley's body was bending down toward his prey. The sobbing man threw a feeble punch at Foley who caught his arm and held it firm. "No! Stop!" Foley screamed to himself. "I won't! I won't!"

"BRAINS!" the horde—only a few steps from him—howled.

Foley felt his jaw open. "Oh god forgive me." The man's forearm tasted squishy at first. Foley's teeth sliced through meat and vein as if a knife through butter.

"BRAINS!"

The horde had descended. Foley felt his prey jerk as a female corpse grabbed the man's head and began smashing it against a rock lying underneath him. "BRAINS!"

"STOP!" Foley begged himself, to no avail. Pieces of warm forearm slid down his gullet. Foley felt the warm, bloody flesh slide all the way into his growling stomach.

CRACK.

The sound of the man's skull breaking open against the rock made Foley's body look up from his meal.

"Brains," the dead woman said while looking straight at Foley and scooping up the gelatinous goo in her clawlike fingers. She raised the bloody goop to her mouth, slurping it greedily.

⟫⟨⟩⟪

"We're losing her!" Shelbi barked out.

"No! We're saving her!" Grandma growled back at Shelbi.

"She's losing too much blood," Shelbi responded while rifling through a drawer. "Got it." She held up a scalpel. "We're going to save the baby."

"You're going to save both of them!"

Shelbi had known Grandma for fifteen years. She knew how dangerous Jane was—it was why she had befriended Jane right away. Shelbi knew that if Jaime died the old woman would shoot her.

"I'm saving the child first." Shelbi's eyes burned at Grandma. "Hold her down."

Jaime began convulsing on the table. "There's rope in the cabinet behind you! We have to tie her down. I have to do a C-section."

Grandma turned away, rushed toward the cabinet, and found the rope. Shelbi jabbed a syringe into the dying woman's throat and whispered, "That'll speed this up." She kissed Jaime's cold, sweaty forehead and tenderly whispered, "Good-bye."

⟫⟨⟩⟪

Foley's body rose up from its meal. The warm chunks of flesh slid through his intestines and began leaking out of him, sliding down his legs as he stood. "I didn't do that," he told himself. "I can't control this."

149

"Come with me my brother," a voice behind him called out. Foley heard footsteps running toward him from behind. He felt a hand grasp his left shoulder and then spin him around.

"Don't fight it brother." The fast corpse who turned him around quickly stepped back from Foley. "Just let go brother. Don't fight it, you're already dead. Why not have a little fun before you fall over?"

The fast corpse circled Foley as he talked. "It's easy. Let go and just enjoy it. You're dead anyway. Why not have some fun?"

BAM BAM.

"Gunshots." The fast corpse was giddy. "Gunshots mean fun." The corpse looked at Foley and said, "Join me, let's go kill." It turned and began racing down the dirt path toward the sound of the gunfire.

———

"Save my baby!" Jaime's scream was ear piercing. "Save her!"

Even though Jaime was lashed to the table, Grandma still had to pin down her shoulders. Her body thrashed to free itself as Shelbi plunged the scalpel into her stomach and began cutting.

Grandma had tuned out the horrifying screams Jaime's freshly dead corpse was emitting. Her mind focused on only one thing. The baby.

Grandma watched Shelbi cut open Jaime's belly and said, "Please God. Please help. Please...I'll do anything."

Shelbi reached into the dead woman's womb. She raised the baby out of Jaime and slapped the child on the bottom. Grandma started crying as she heard the child wail out. "Is she?"

"He," Shelbi replied. "He is alive and he is perfect." She held the child up for Grandma to see.

Grandma felt a wave of terror crawl across her skin. She could hear them approaching in the distance. "Jaime's screaming must've attracted them," she thought. She looked at Shelbi, then at the newborn squirming in her arms. "Take care of him, Shelbi."

"What?" Shelbi replied.

"I've done enough damage to this family." She looked down at the newborn. "Name him Michael after my baby brother."

"Wait, what are you doing?" Shelbi replied, faking panic. "You can't go out there."

"Promise me you'll call him Michael," the tearful woman snapped back as she headed toward the door. She grabbed Shelbi's twelve-gauge shotgun off a gun rack next to a picture of her and Shelbi with the president of New England. "Promise me!"

"I promise," Shelbi said as Grandma exited for battle. "I promise."

⌐⌐⌐

Foley staggered slowly in the direction of the gunfire, following the same path as the fast corpse.

"You should've listened to him," his mind whispered in his ear. "Let go, you can feel your body aching to let loose." The fast corpse had been right about his body. Since the encounter Foley's gait had changed. At first his body had been numb and beyond his control. After the corpse had confronted him he began to feel his legs—it felt as though thousands of small pinpricks were racing up and down them. The intensity of the pain grew as the pinpricks spread upward across Foley's skin. It grew from the feeling of an asleep limb waking up to the pain of walking face first into an angry hornets' nest.

Then: a miracle.

Every bit of pain left him. Foley felt exhilaration in being able to "feel" himself. He looked down and saw part of his torso was missing, but he felt no pain. His first steps were steady. And they felt great. Euphoria swept every infested fiber of his carcass. He took his first step under his own will. Then a second. Foley felt power surging through his limbs.

"Kill."

That thought. That one word, delivered to his mind with such glee, snapped him back. "No," he replied to the thought as he willed his body to halt.

"Kill."

"Stop." But it wouldn't. It faltered, it staggered. The feeling of being attacked by hornets returned with a vengeance. "Stop! God damn it stop!" Every inch of his skin erupted in agony. The carcass wouldn't stop. But he had managed to slow it down to its original speed. As he fought for control of the rotting piece of meat propelling him each slow and staggering step became more excruciating than the last.

"Why are we fighting this?"

"Shut up!" Foley's body quickly lunged forward. The pain vanished and a surge of power swept through his body.

"NO!" The meat suit staggered half a step sideways. Pain raced up and down Foley's carcass. The hole in his torso was colder than any winter. "I'M NOT GOING TO KILL !," he screamed to himself as his carcass returned to its slow and painful stagger.

"Cut it out."

"I am not going to kill."

"What's the point of this? Just give in, stop the pain."

"No. Stop talking to yourself."

Seriously? You really think that's going to work? What did Grandma used to call that? The power of positive thinking.

Foley staggered as he momentarily lost control of the hungry carcass. The pain that was returning, while hideous, was also reassuring to Foley. "Just keep riding the brakes." As long as he hurt, he had some control.

"Why are you putting yourself through this?"

"Keep riding the brakes."

"Your plan can't work. Just give in. Be evil. Have some fun before you rot and fall apart."

"I'm not evil."

"Yes you are. You can fool yourself. But you can't fool me."

"I am not evil."

"Just stop it. Don't you remember?"

"What?"

"When it was all over, remember now? The birds? The lady?"

Foley remembered. The images from fifteen years ago were so vivid that he felt the snowflakes falling on him as he walked toward a flock of birds.

The sky over the ocean was black with ravens. The murder of crows, as Grandma called it, began amassing a week after the dead were defeated. Within three days there were more birds than Foley had ever seen. The water along the shore was filled with the debris left over from civilization; it was also filled with bloated, putrid body parts that attracted scavenging birds by the thousands. Jaime's voice from when they were children rang in his ears: "I found one!" Foley jumped off the twisted wreckage of a Buick and raced along the riverbank toward her excited voice. "It's just a head." Jaime said.

Foley remembered the rage that coursed through his child-size body that day. He remembered the sight of that thing staring at him while wedged between an upended birch tree and a wheel that had snapped off a car.

"Foley, no!" Jaime screamed—but it did no good. He pounced on the decapitated head. He could feel the scalp start to tear away from the skull as his hands ripped out clumps of hair from the monster, which was snapping at him.

"No!" Jaime said and threw him off of the skull, which was still wedged in its spot, minus two clumps of scalp. "It can still bite you."

"It killed Jaden." Foley knew this particular lady's skull wasn't the one that had torn his brother to shreds in front of him at the

153

camp. But it was one of them. To his five-year-old mind that was the same thing. He knew he wanted to hurt it like it had hurt Jaden. "I want to kill it!"

"OK," Jaime said. Her voice was soothing. "Let me make it safe first." Her hand touched his shoulder. The young girl scoured the riverbank until she found the perfect mouth-size rock. She hurled the stone into the monster's snapping jaws. The force of the impact cracking the creatures teeth. The rock now lodged securely in the zombies head, preventing it from moving its jaws an inch. She then nodded at Foley, who lunged at the skull, tearing gray flesh with the efficiency of a piranha. He finally killed it by slowly pushing a stick through its eyeball until it reached the brain.

"Remember her tear?"

"That was fluid from its eyeball popping."

"That was a believable story to tell yourself, until today. You know better now. She was crying."

"I was a kid." Foley's soul felt sick. "I didn't know. How could I have known? It's not my fault."

"It's still your responsibility. You tortured her for hours."

"I didn't know"

"Doesn't matter."

"Yes it does!"

"Not to her."

⇒⊹ ⊹⇐

BAM BAM.

Two shotgun blasts. Two newly headless corpses tumbled backward off Shelbi's porch. "What the fuck are you doing?" Grandma thought. She knew she had made a tactical error. She had reacted without thinking and now the woods around the house erupted with the sound of the screaming dead. "So fucking stupid." Four cadavers staggered out of the woods and onto the lawn. "Why didn't I smash in their skulls?" She was thinking about the carcasses on the porch. She could have taken them out quickly and quietly. She easily could've smashed their faces in with the butt of the shotgun. Instead she had shot them, drawing more monsters to her position.

"Only one thing to do." Grandma began charging straight at the screaming bodies that were stumbling toward her. "Can't draw anymore in." She knew as she ran toward them that she wasn't going to make it through this battle. She felt it in her bones—this was it. The first of the four screaming corpses was in striking distance. It was Laurie. Grandma remembered the first time she met Laurie back in the camps—how strong she was, how resilient.

THWACK!

Laurie's face collapsed as the shotgun stock crushed in her left eye socket. Grandma spun from Laurie's collapsing body, smashing Fred's face, the man who taught people how to farm and how to survive. The bones in his face gave a hideous crunch as he fell. Two more screamers were almost on her. *BAM BAM.* Two clean headshots—the last corpses fell. Grandma turned to her right. She screamed "Shelbi!" as she saw her dearest friend in the world cradling her newborn grandson in her left arm, and pointing a gun at her with her right.

BAM!

Grandma's knee exploded. She collapsed, her shotgun falling from her hand as fell. The ground came up fast on her. Her head bounced off the rocky soil with the force of a car collision. She looked toward Shelbi, her mind unable to grasp what had truly happened, until she saw Shelbi smile at her before getting into Grandma's car with little Michael and leaving.

More screaming from behind her. Grandma, in an ever-increasing pool of her own blood, began crawling toward the shotgun that was four feet away. "Eat the barrel," she thought. "Just end it. You've failed at every turn." The screaming sound grew louder every second as a carcass approached her from her side.

"Please god, let me get to the gun." She was pleading out loud. "Please god please let me get to the gun, I can't become one of them."

Her left hand strained to reach the barrel and drew the weapon close. Her right hand grabbed the stock and jammed it against the grass. Using the weapon for leverage, she raised herself up high enough to put her mouth in the barrel. Her left hand wrapped around the barrel, her fingers on her right struggling to reach the trigger, she glanced to her left and saw a snarling, screaming Foley approaching.

⚊⊰⊱⚊

"Shoot!" Foley screamed as he painfully staggered toward the woman who had raised him as if he were her own. "Shoot before I reach you."

Grandma couldn't quite reach the trigger. She looked at Foley approaching and realized what had to be done. She had to save him from this. She should have done it back at the house, she knew that. She could get off a shot at Foley, then she could take care of herself. She took the barrel out of her mouth, fell to the ground, and took a wild shot at Foley all in the blink of an eye. The weapon's kickback sent her reeling. The gun flew from her hands. Looking up, she saw she had once again failed. She missed. Foley was almost on her, that horrible shriek pounding in her ears.

"She missed me!" Despair choked Foley.

"Kill her."

The voice taunting him to kill gave him an idea. "Brains." Suddenly he understood. "Brains. Eat her brains." It was the only way. "Eat her brains, save her from this."

Grandma, lying in a pool of her own blood, was now sobbing. "I DESERVE THIS !" she screamed at Foley's corpse. "I don't blame you. This is my fault. I deserve this."

"Brains! Eat her brains."

"I've never done anything but destroy and hurt my family," Grandma said while sobbing. "I'm worthless. I deserve this."

Foley didn't feel the tears flowing down his face while his teeth were scraping the scalp of his screaming grandmother's head.

"I deserve this," she thought while feeling his teeth gnawing at her skull.

"This isn't working," Foley thought. He couldn't open his mouth wide enough to get a crushing bite. His teeth were just scraping the same skull-exposed spot over and over with no progress.

"Your jaw isn't strong enough to crack her open."

The voice torturing Foley at every turn was right. "Do something fast before she turns!" Foley's hand was clutching Grandma by the ear. "Smash her skull open." He saw an exposed oak tree root lying under them while his jaw kept scraping and scraping. With every ounce of his strength he commanded himself: "SAVE HER!!!" His arm began bashing her head against the hard oak root. The first hit cracked her skull in half. The second hit it split wide open, her brains leaking out of the gaping wound. Foley dove for the brain, slurping them up as they leaked from her broken cranium.

Foley felt elated. He saved her. He kept her from turning.

"This is delicious."

The voice taunting him made him wish he could throw up.

"Really, really delicious. Consistency, somewhere between jelly and ice cream I'd say. But the taste is really close to bacon."

"Fuck you."

"Oh how poetic."

"Fuck you." Foley thought again as the last delicious bit of brain matter slid down his gullet. "I won that. I saved her."

"Really? She looks dead to me."

"I saved her from turning."

"Whatever gets you through, but in my book dead is dead. Whether you walk around hungry after you die or not, you're still dead."

Foley heard shrieking coming from Shelbi's house. His body turned toward the sound of the undead wailing, drawn as if a moth to a flame. He recognized the voice. Jaime was in there, and she was screaming "My baby!" over and over and over.

Foley staggered up the porch stairs and through the open door. Jaime was strapped down with her stomach splayed open. Blood and organs had poured out of her like a waterfall, coating the floor with a sticky crimson pool of drying refuse.

She saw Foley as he approached and began sobbing.

"The baby is safe." Foley lied to her.

"I can hear you!" Jaime's head was swimming. "How can I hear you?"

"Don't know," he replied.

"The baby!" Jaime pleaded.

Foley did the only thing he could, he lied. "I saw Grandma take off with the baby. They are both safe."

Relief washed over Jaime's mutilated corpse. "Did Shelbi make it?"

"Don't know."

"How bad is it?" she asked.

"It's isolated." He lied again. "The army is winning."

"He's beautiful. Grandma asked Shelbi to call him Michael."

"That's a great name."

The two corpses stayed in that shack until the end. For six week Foley refused to leave Jaime, no matter how hard his body ached to move, no matter how hungry, nothing moved him from his love's side. Even after the maggots ate away the soft tissue of his eyes and he couldn't see her, he stayed. The vermin stole his hearing and his voice the same way. Finally, mercifully, the maggots ate away his cerebral cortex and he was gone.

Jaime's final journey was the same: slowly being devoured by grubs, maggots, and beetles. She lasted longer than Foley and watched him fall and die. She faced her demise with dignity and serenity knowing that at least her baby was safe.

⪪+⪫

"Who's a good little boy?" Shelbi cooed at little Michael in the front seat of the car as they drove away from Grandma. "You are, that's who."

The child was squirming until Shelbi put her right hand on his tummy, gently securing him.

The drive down the dirt path to her old home was quick—less than five minutes. From there it was a quick walk to the bunker entrance, hidden in the side of the mountain.

As she carried the newborn down into her old lair, she was hit with an overwhelming sense of nostalgia. Seemed like it was only yesterday when she and Michael first put down roots in these Western Massachusetts woods. The two of them were so full of dreams. Saving humanity from itself. Ending war and poverty and establishing a new and lasting world order with Michael's brilliance guiding humanity toward a divine and righteous path.

"How did it all go to shit?" Shelbi thought.

The hallway toward the old lab was dark. Shelbi had hooked up a few small solar panels, hidden in the woods, to provide enough power for a few lights.

"Time for you two to meet," Shelbi said and threw open the door to the lab. Her former lover and current God's body floated weightlessly in the formaldehyde-filled Martyr Tank. The failed experiments having long been removed from the tank, Michael's severely damaged corpse opened its mouth, the formaldehyde silencing his screaming as much as the thick acrylic aquarium walls.

Only Michael's upper body resided in the tank. His long silver hair resembled tentacles as it floated and twisted inside the acrylic womb he was encased in. The rattlesnake strikes along his face, arms, and chest had eaten away at his flesh thanks to the digestive enzymes contained in the venom, leaving gaps in his flesh that exposed bone and sinew. Where his skin was still covering his body, a sickly purplish-gray hue colored the flesh with death. The intestines hanging out from his stomach looked like jellyfish tendrils. Michael's corpse snapped its jaws at the newborn she held.

"Look, Father is trying to say hello," Shelbi said.

Michael snapped his dead jaws again at the pair in front of him. "KILL ME!!! KILL ME!!! KILL ME!!!"

For fifteen years he had been pleading with her for his death. Instead she put him in this hermetically sealed, formaldehyde-filled tomb.

"PLEASE!!! KILL ME!!!" Michael thought.

"So I bet you're wondering why I brought you a visitor," Shelbi said. Her voice lilted as though talking to a child as she addressed her God. "The gift found a way. After all this time. After all the radiation the gift found a way."

The chemical-filled womb Michael floated in prevented him from hearing Shelbi. He watched as she held the baby up and smiled. He couldn't hear a word she was saying and he didn't care. All he wanted was to die.

"PLEASE!!!" Michael thought.

"After fifteen long years, it came back." Her face beamed with pride. "The gift is back. It's destroying the last of the sinners now."

Michael stared at her. She had been so beautiful once. He had loved her so deeply. And now when he saw her he felt hatred—hatred for not killing him, hatred for keeping him here like a pet, and hatred for believing he was God.

"Now," Shelbi said while turning the squirming newborn to the side, "you can see where his ears are bleeding. When I left your sister behind I shot her kneecap out. The sound probably ruptured his eardrums." She bounced the child in her arms. "I'm not sure if little Michael died then or not, but definitely within a few minutes."

She turned away from the tank and carried the dead newborn toward a table. "I am sure this child holds the key to your regeneration." She placed little Michael face first on the steel table, picked up a scalpel, and began dissecting him. "This baby was born during the outbreak. I believe his spinal fluid may hold the key to everything." Michael couldn't hear the madness in her voice—he floated hopelessly in his prison as she sliced the child to bits, "Once I get you back everything will work out," she said to her God.

And Michael watched. He watched her experiment over and over again on the samples from the baby. He watched as days turned into months, then years. He watched as Shelbi got older and sicker. He saw her fall over dead from a heart attack not knowing it had been five years since she had brought the child to him and twenty years since he gave the world the gift—to him it felt like ten thousand years. The lights in the bunker failed two weeks after Shelbi died, leaving Michael in complete darkness.

All of Michael's followers had succumbed to the fast dead long ago in the first outbreak. The last outbreak had killed every last remaining human on the planet.

He never knew that he had won. Earth was free from war, hunger, racism, and all of man's evils because it had been freed from humanity.

Except for Michael. One immortal consciousness, perfectly preserved in his formaldehyde tomb... left alone and scared... screaming in the darkness...,...for eternity.

Made in the USA
Charleston, SC
27 July 2015